First Paperback edition published, 2025

ISBN: 978-1-951722-14-2 eBook

ISBN: 978-1-951722-15-9 Paperback

For my darling daughter, Marta
For my supportive husband, Peter

Contents

CHAPTER 1

Cora and Brian stepped onto the observation deck of the luxurious Spencer Space Station. This spherical, floating station served as a vacation destination for Askovs—family members of Askovians who had evolved into humans with special abilities.

"When do you think it'll start?" Cora asked. She had bronze skin and shoulder-length curly hair, wearing a casual tan-and-green-striped short-sleeved top and matching dark-brown pants. She glanced over the half-filled circular deck before turning to gaze through the clear dome overhead at the stars, then down at Earth.

"Should be a few more minutes," Brian said, his blue-gray eyes meeting hers. He was dressed casually in a white top and black pants. He reached for her hand, and they exchanged glances.

The space station maintained Earth gravity for its visitors using alythium, a crystal mined from the moons of Earth, Mars, and Jupiter. It orbited four hundred kilometers above Earth's equatorial surface about fifteen times a day.

"I wish we could see the actual plasma from the sun," she said. They wove through a maze of chairs and tables until they found one near the edge of the room, bordered by a railing that prevented people from touching the clear dome. The railing also obstructed their view of Earth.

"We'll see its effects when it collides with Earth's atmosphere," he said.

Cora and Brian settled into their seats and ordered drinks from the meal crafter. The device transported food and beverages from a nearby pantry by converting matter to energy and then back to matter as the items appeared on the table. Cora ordered a fruity mango drink, while Brian opted for tea with a raspberry teacake.

"Oh, somebody's got a pair of those solar flare glasses," she said. "Maybe we should get some."

"I really don't think you'll need them," he replied.

"Mmm..." Cora said, sipping her mango juice. "There's something else in here with the mango. Maybe lemon? It's tangy."

"The glasses help if you want to see the plasma shooting through space," he said, glancing at the little old lady with the viewing glasses. "But honestly, the real beauty of the solar flare comes from how it interacts with Earth's atmosphere. Don't be so impatient." He tugged her arm in a playful gesture.

Brian took a bite of his strawberry-and-cream teacake. He nodded as a slow smile spread across his face.

"To our fifth-month anniversary," Cora said, raising her mango juice. Though they'd only been dating a few months, their relationship felt so comfortable, having known each other for years.

He stood, leaned over the table, and gave her a peck on the lips.

A warm, fuzzy feeling spread through her chest, and they exchanged a grin.

Eventually, he took another bite of his teacake, and she sipped more mango juice.

As Cora scanned the circular room, she noticed several Askovs stepping off the antigrav lift and spilling into the space. Many gravitated toward seats near the edge of the dome, where the view would be spectacular as the station slowly rotated on its axis.

The murmur of the crowd increased, and everyone turned their attention to Earth's atmosphere. A gentle white glow appeared at its outer limits, gradually growing in intensity and changing color. It started as a dull white glow, brightened to a brilliant white, and then shifted to pale green.

"Oh, that's beautiful. I'm so glad we made it here early," Cora said with excitement.

As the atmosphere's interaction intensified, the glow sank further into the firmament. The color deepened to a brighter green with flashes of pink and blue as the event continued.

"Amazing," Brian said, his mouth full of tea-cake. "And these are the best."

Excited chatter filled the space as Cora leaned forward for a better view. She looked at Brian with a broad grin.

"Oh, you..." she chuckled. "Is that all you ever think about?"

"At teatime, I'm afraid to say, yes," he said, wiping his mouth.

"Hundreds of years ago, this plasma storm would've disabled all electrical gadgets. Today, it's just a beautiful event to enjoy."

"It's gorgeous," he agreed. "I wonder what's causing all the different colors?"

"It depends on how the sun's plasma interacts with the gases in the atmosphere."

"How long do you think it'll last?"

"This could go on for hours," she said, peering through the clear dome with excitement.

After about thirty minutes, the crowd thinned, and the chatter quieted.

"Oh, look, we're still in time to see it," an attractive woman in her mid-twenties said. She had brown hair and blue-green eyes.

Cora glanced at a nearby man with the same blue-green eyes. She thought they might be siblings.

Most people on the space station were Askovs or Askovians. As a Feeler, Cora could sense others' emotions. However, with the crowded observation deck, she shielded her mind to avoid being overwhelmed by a flood of feelings.

"Willow, you're the only one I know who'd be interested in this everyday phenomenon," the gentleman said.

"This doesn't happen all the time," Willow said. "Besides, you know you're enjoying it, too. You just like to complain so you don't have to admit you like science as much as I do."

He chuckled.

"Were you dragged up here by a science enthusiast, too?" Brian asked, turning to the brown-haired man.

"Yeah. She's been this way since we were kids," the brown-haired man replied, his blue-green eyes twinkling. "I'm Arthur, by the way."

"Brian and Cora," Brian said, gesturing to his partner.

"This is my sister, Willow," Arthur said.

"How are you enjoying the show?" Willow asked.

"I love the amazing colors from Earth's atmosphere," Cora said. "I could stay here all day, but I think the show will be over in about an hour."

"So, you're a science enthusiast like my sister," Arthur said. "All I've been hearing about this week is solar flares, coronal mass ejections, plasma, and on and on." He rolled his eyes dramatically as his sister nudged him playfully.

"I think it's beautiful," Brian said. "Especially if you're an artist. These greens and blues would be fascinating to capture. It's hard to imagine how nature creates such amazing colors."

"Are you a Spencer?" Willow asked. "Every year, I come to the Spencer Industries' State of the Company address, and I meet new cousins."

"No, we're here on vacation," Cora replied.

"I'd heard about the company address," Brian said, exchanging a glance with Cora. "But we had other plans."

"Be thankful you missed it," Arthur said with a chuckle. "But you're in the right spot for a vacation. The space station has a lot of amenities. What've you done so far?"

"Nothing much. We only arrived yesterday," Cora said. "But I definitely plan to have a full spa day."

"And you?" Arthur asked, turning to Brian.

"And I definitely plan to not have a full spa day," Brian said with a joking tone. "Instead, I'll be spending as much time as possible by the beach and pool."

"I agree with that plan," Arthur said. "If you want company, let us know. Willow and I spend most of our time at the beach."

"The engineering behind having an entire ocean in space is amazing," Cora said with a bright smile. "We're taking a tour called The Making of the Space Station later."

"Oh, we've taken that tour before," Willow said. "It's a little boring because they dumbed it down too much."

"Too bad," Cora said with a slight frown. "I was looking forward to it."

"So, was the State of the Company address interesting?" Brian asked.

Arthur laughed, and Willow shrugged.

"My goal was to stay awake as long as possible," Arthur replied.

"We're required to attend every year," Willow said. "I suppose we should understand where our income comes from, though."

"The vacation after the State of the Company address must be a good reward," Cora said.

Everyone laughed.

An hour later, Cora and Brian stepped onto the space station's Pool Deck from the antigrav lifts. These lifts filled the space station's central column, making it possible to travel to all fifty-seven floors.

The Pool Deck offered every possible way to enjoy water without a beach. There were four large pools of varying depths. Hoards of screaming kids filled the shallow pool, which was located near one corner of the deck, isolated from the remaining three pools.

"What do you think about swimming?" Brian asked, strolling toward two large pools in the middle of the deck. Adults gravitated toward these pools. The fourth pool, separated from the others on the opposite side of the deck, was much deeper and featured a twisty waterslide and a cacophony of screaming adults and children.

"I've been thinking about it," Cora said, following him as they passed seven hot tubs and numerous lounge chairs, tables, and bars. "But there's something I need to do. I promised Aunt Ferna a vidchat when we arrived, but I didn't do it yesterday. If I contact her now, could we meet up a little later? That way, you could swim now."

"It'll be a sacrifice being here all by myself," he said with a false somber tone, which didn't quite pull off because of his half-smile. "But I'll make the sacrifice and go swimming."

Cora gave him a gentle nudge on his shoulder. They exchanged a quick kiss, and she turned to head back to their room. She took the antigrav lift to their floor and stepped out into the hallway.

Her comm bracelet chimed, and she received an urgent vidchat from Evan Pendleton. The comm connected the wearer to Earth's Global High-Frequency Network, known as the Net, which spanned Earth, the Spencer Space Station, and Lunar City.

I wonder what he wants, she thought. He never contacts me directly. She glanced around the empty hallway and answered the chat.

A floating window appeared over her bracelet, and Evan Pendleton's image filled the screen. He was a broad man with reddish, graying hair and intelligent blue eyes—features common to most Pendletons.

"Cora, I'm sorry to interrupt your vacation," Evan said. "But something serious has come up. I know you don't owe me any favors, but I'm asking you to please help Ivy Santos."

"What's going on? Is she in trouble?" Cora asked, a sinking feeling forming in the pit of her stomach.

"She may be in trouble with the EGS," he said, his face pinched. The Earth Global Security (EGS) was Earth's police force. "In the past, you've helped others with issues, murder specifically. Please tell me you can help Ivy."

Cora wrapped her arms around her torso while her floating screen remained in place.

"How did you even know I was here?" she asked.

"I called Ferna first. She told me how to find you," Evan replied. "Don't get angry with Ferna. She explained you're on vacation and might not be too available." He paused and turned toward something off-screen. "The EGS hasn't charged Ivy yet, but I'm afraid I won't be able to keep her safe. My Askovian powers won't protect her if the EGS finds either of us guilty."

Cora thought for a moment about the wonderful time she and Brian had shared on their one day of vacation. She'd finally been able to relax, knowing no one was trying to kill her. Her first instinct was to say no, but she remembered Ivy—sweet, struggling Ivy, a painter trying to make her way among other Askovs. Cora had seen her paintings at the Alinac Gallery, and she couldn't bring herself to say no.

"Can you tell me what's going on?" Cora asked.

"No, not now," Evan said. "I'll need you to come to my suite. The EGS is monitoring everything, and I need to talk to you in private."

"When would you like to talk?"

"As soon as possible. I don't know how much more time Ivy will have." He sighed. "Hopefully, I'm overreacting and she'll be safe, but I just don't trust them."

"All right, I'll come now," she said, and the screen went dark.

She quickly sent a message to Brian, explaining that something had come up with Evan Pendleton. She told him she'd fill him in later.

If he's already swimming, he won't see the message for a while, she thought with a sigh, wishing she could join him.

CHAPTER 2

Several minutes later, Cora strolled to the door of Evan Pendleton's suite. It slid open, and she stepped in, only to freeze. An EGS agent stood as she entered and introduced himself.

"Good afternoon, Ms. Brimble," a short, muscular, red-headed EGS agent said, dressed in a brown jumpsuit.

Cora nodded, glancing at Evan with a quizzical expression. *Didn't he say he wanted to meet in private?* she thought.

She almost raised her shield but remembered that EGS agents wore neurowalls. These tech implants shielded their minds from Askovians, like Readers and Feelers. Readers could detect others' thoughts, but the neurowalls made life easier for Cora since the agents' random emotions wouldn't bother her.

"I'm Agent Tate," he said. "Mr. Pendleton is not under arrest, but we've asked him to stay on the space station for now." He turned to the second EGS agent. "This is Agent Reed."

Reed, a tall, muscular woman in the EGS brown jumpsuit, nodded. She wore her blonde hair pulled back into a tight bun.

"Evan, what's going on?" Cora asked, stepping into the living room and dining room combination. The space reminded her of the furniture in Lunar City—lavish but in shades of gray and brown. The living room featured two large, gray sofas across from each other, with an oversized coffee table between. A set of overstuffed, gray chairs also sat opposite each other between the two sofas. Artwork hung on the walls that resembled pieces she'd seen at the Alinac Gallery.

"Sorry, they showed up right after our chat," Evan said.

Cora lowered herself onto the same sofa where Evan was sitting, while the two EGS agents took seats on the sofa opposite.

"We're here to show the vids of Ms. Spencer's death to Mr. Pendleton," Agent Tate said in a stiff voice. "As a courtesy to him, we waited for you. We'd appreciate any of your insights."

"Ms. Spencer? You mean Jessica?" Cora asked, raising her eyebrows. "What do you mean—murder? What happened?" Jessica Spencer was the head of Spencer Industries, with graying brown hair and a pinched face. Cora glanced at Evan again, sensing strong waves of sadness from him.

"Let's get started," Agent Reed said in a cool, detached tone. "We've reviewed the vids, and this is the period before the murder. You'll see Jessica Spencer sitting alone at her desk."

On a large floating screen, Cora watched Jessica move her fingers back and forth between four floating windows.

"Note the display of religious knives at the corner of her desk," Tate said.

At the edge of the floating screen, a pedestal with three ornate, floating knives appeared, fanned out to show intricate carvings on each handle.

"We'll switch to a new view showing Ms. Spencer and most of the living room," Reed said. "You can see Ms. Spencer turning around, but she doesn't appear surprised. We can't tell if she sees someone or something because the view stops just before the door."

"Is there another view of the door only?" Cora asked.

"Yes," Reed said, using her fingers to manipulate the screen and showing a new angle of the door from the inside. "The door opens and closes, but nobody's there."

"I've seen that before," Cora said with a shiver.

"We heard about Mr. Varney in Lunar City," Agent Tate said. "He used military tech to hide from our monitors. We've sent a request to headquarters to check into this."

Reed changed the view again to show Jessica facing the door. "From this angle, we can't tell if she's talking to someone," she said, pointing to Jessica, who had turned slightly away from the monitors. "But pay attention to the knives. The largest knife in the display jumps off the table, floats through the air, and stabs her in the chest, piercing her heart."

Cora cringed when the knife plunged into Jessica. Wrapping her arms tight around herself, she held her breath as she watched Jessica fall forward.

"Death was instantaneous," Reed said.

Cora sensed fresh waves of Evan's pain and almost raised her shield, but it subsided.

"I've never seen anything like that," she said in a hoarse voice. "I've seen other people die, but not like that." She shivered.

"I'm so sorry to put you through this," Evan said in a sympathetic tone. "I didn't know what was in the vids before the EGS arrived. Otherwise, I would've asked them not to show them to you."

Cora sensed Evan's sincerity.

"I don't understand. Why do you think Evan had anything to do with this?" Cora asked.

Agent Reed continued the vid. "I'll forward a few minutes," she said. "The door slides open, and you see Mr. Pendleton and Ms. Santos."

Cora watched Evan rush to Jessica's side while Ivy screamed. Ivy was a young woman in her twenties with light-brown, wavy hair. She covered her mouth and stood frozen in the middle of the floor.

"Mr. Pendleton shakes Ms. Spencer and puts his hand on the knife," Reed said. "Why did you touch the knife?"

"I really don't know," Evan said, shrugging his shoulder. "I was in shock and tried to do something..."

Cora sensed his deep despair and wondered at it. She thought they hated each other.

"Now Mr. Nicholas Perry enters," Reed said. Nick Perry appeared to be in his late thirties or early forties, with blond hair and blue eyes. Cora recognized his flawless physique—he'd been genetically modified for appearance. Many Askov families took advantage of this technology to produce attractive children, making it easier for them to choose a spouse. He strolled into the living room, rubbing his eyes and wearing a rumpled white shirt and shorts.

I wonder how old he really is? Cora thought. He seemed to be Jessica's lover, and he was in her bedroom.

"What's happening?" Nick said on the vid. He paused, struggling to take in the scene of two people in the living room. His gaze then fell on Jessica. "No, no, no," he said while sprinting to her body. He pushed Evan to the side and shook Jessica. Then he fell over her body, sobbing.

Cora's heart squeezed at his distraught sobs. He sounded genuinely upset.

Evan wiped his eyes and scooted away from Nick. He stood, gave Ivy a gentle hug, and guided her to the nearest chair. It made Cora wonder about the relationship between those two.

The floating screen froze, showing Evan comforting Ivy and Nick crying over Jessica.

"Now you've seen the events leading up to and after Ms. Spencer's death," Agent Tate said. "What are your thoughts?"

"I... I don't know," Cora said, blinking at the frozen screen.

"I think we're both in too much shock to be useful right now," Evan said, blinking back tears.

"Were either you or Ms. Santos in the suite earlier in the morning?" Tate asked.

"Of course not," Evan said. "What are you implying?"

"But nothing in these vids shows Evan or Ivy had anything to do with Jessica's death," Cora said, furrowing her brows.

"We're following our procedures," Agent Tate said. "They work when we don't deviate from the steps."

Cora crossed her arms and furrowed her brows further.

"Right now, you, Mr. Pendleton, and Ms. Santos are the only non-EGS agents who know Ms. Spencer is dead," he said. "We asked them to remain confined to their cabins for six hours, giving us time to process some of the evidence from the crime scene."

"How long do you want me to keep quiet?" she asked.

"Six hours have already passed," he replied. "That's why we could show you the vids."

"She's been dead for six hours already?" Cora asked. "Have you notified her sister yet?"

"Other agents are performing those tasks," Agent Tate replied. He paused, exchanging a glance with Agent Reed. "I just want to emphasize something, Ms. Brimble," he said. "We do not want your help. I've heard from Agents Taylor, Donaldson, and Lewis. It doesn't appear that your help is always useful. Please do not involve yourself in our investigation."

He turned to Agent Reed, who had closed the floating screen. They nodded to Evan and left the suite.

Cora quietly examined Evan's tumbling emotions. Eventually, he managed them, and they didn't overwhelm her.

"I'm sorry for your loss," Cora said in a gentle voice. She didn't understand why Evan was so affected, but she felt he needed emotional support.

Evan cleared his throat several times and said, "Thank you."

"Is there something else you'd like to add about Jessica's death?" Cora asked.

"No, not at this point," he said in a thick voice. "I think we have to wait for their investigation. Anyway, I called you because of Ivy. Would you befriend her? I don't trust the EGS, and there may be a time I won't be able to protect her."

"Do you think they'll try to arrest you?" she asked.

"Possibly," he shrugged. "I don't know."

Cora reflected on the confrontation she'd had with the Cartwrights—Hazel and her mom, Winifred, both powerful Movers just like Evan.

"What I don't understand is what's preventing you from packing up Ivy and leaving right now?" she asked.

Evan chuckled. "Ivy still has to live on Earth," he said. "I don't want her to exist like the Cartwrights."

Cora raised her eyebrows at the mention of Hazel and Winifred Cartwright.

CHAPTER 3

The following day, Cora and Brian sat in the Planetary Café on the space station's shopping level. The space station maintained the same time as Tymal, since most Askovs flew to the space station from that city. In reality, the space station orbited Earth about fifteen times a day, so they needed a way to maintain some semblance of day and night. They chose Tymal's time zone.

"I can't believe she's dead," Brian said, taking a sip of his tea. "It feels as if I spoke to her just a few days ago."

They sat among a sea of tables with two to four chairs each, covering the café floor. Images of Earth, Mars, and Jupiter filled the walls, while muted instrumental music played softly in the background.

"What bothers me most is the way she died," Cora said, a shiver running down her spine. "It seemed cold and calculating."

The café was a popular spot because of the stunning views through a series of portals on one wall. At certain parts of the day, the portals filled with bright pinpoint stars, Earth's continents and oceans, or the moon's craters.

"I'm sorry Agent Tate showed that vid to you," Brian said, gently grasping her hand. "Did Evan really not know what the EGS was going to do?"

"Yeah, he seemed just as surprised as I was."

"Seems Ivy's running late."

"I wonder if she's still upset."

"Well, at least we have a gorgeous view," he said, taking a bite of a raspberry teacake.

"I have to say, the coffee's good here," she said after taking a sip.

"What do you want to do? I mean, as far as our vacation. I know you plan to befriend Ivy, but it doesn't feel like we've started our break yet."

"Yeah, you're right. But I'm hoping the EGS will do their job, find the killer, and let the rest of us get on with our lives." She gave him a lopsided smile.

"I suppose it's good to be positive," he said.

"Maybe the pool—" she began, but stopped when she spotted Ivy and Nick entering the café with somber expressions. Brian waved them over, and they made their way around the tables toward them.

Ivy, with shoulder-length light-brown hair, paced toward them in a loose-fitting blue dress that swayed around her legs. Nick followed in a form-fitting blue-and-white-striped shirt.

"Ivy, how are you this morning?" Cora asked, standing and moving toward her.

"I'm fine," Ivy said, grasping Cora's outstretched hand. "I was a bit shaken yesterday, but I'm better now. This is Nick," she said, turning to him. "It's okay. You can trust Cora."

Nick nodded to Cora and Brian, offering a wan smile. Everyone took a seat.

Cora had shielded herself before entering the café, but now she lowered it just a little and focused on Nick. She felt deep waves of sorrow before restoring her mind's protection.

Maybe he really loved Jessica, Cora thought.

"I'm truly sorry for your loss," she said in a solemn voice.

His eyes welled with tears. Ivy leaned toward him and wrapped her arms around his shoulders.

"Is it too soon?" Ivy asked in a quavery voice. "We can meet Cora and Brian later."

"No, I want to get started," Nick said, clearing his throat. "The longer we wait, the more time the killer has to get away."

"How do you two know each other?" Brian asked, putting his empty plate in the recycling.

"I was his student in art school," Ivy said, offering a small smile.

"She was the best student I ever taught," Nick said.

"No—" Ivy protested.

"I mean it," Nick said, interrupting her. "You should see the number of awards she's won for her art."

Ivy turned pink.

"I know yesterday was a terrible day for both of you," Brian said abruptly. "But what do you want from Cora?"

"The EGS thinks I did it," Ivy said. "I found the body."

"No, they think I did it," Nick said, pursing his lips. "I slept while someone..."

"Evan asked me to help yesterday," Cora said. "He said the EGS thinks he did it. What's probably happened is they're questioning you, assuming you're guilty. I've endured their questioning in the past. But they don't have enough information to lead their investigation in any direction. At least, not yet."

"Well, at least that's some good news," Ivy said. "We've got time."

"We'd like you to look into Jessica's death," Nick said, sitting up straighter, as if bracing for her response. "Ivy's told me about your previous investigations, and I think you're better than the EGS."

"I'll tell you what I told Evan," Cora said. "I don't want to get involved in another murder because people continue to die, and then my life's put in danger. I just want to enjoy my vacation.

"D—Uncle Evan said you'd help us," Ivy said.

"I promised him I'd keep an eye on you and help if he's not able to," Cora said gently.

"Well, that's essentially the same thing," Ivy said.

"No. No, it's not," Nick said, frowning. "Someone dangerous is hiding on this station. If they were willing to kill Jessica, the head of the largest mining company in the solar system, what would they do to someone actively hunting them?"

"So, you're going to wait until the killer attacks again?" Ivy asked, leaning onto the table. "What if it's Uncle Evan? Me?"

"I know you were expecting more from me," Cora said, grasping Ivy's hand. "When you hunt a killer, they become scared and do the only thing they know how to do—kill. I already know this is too dangerous."

Ivy pulled her hands from Cora's grasp, crossed her arms, and huffed.

"People could die because of my involvement," Cora said, her eyebrows drawing together. "I don't want that on my conscience, either."

Nick turned to Ivy. "Cora's right. She's on vacation, and we should respect that."

Ivy sighed and seemed to deflate.

"I'm truly sorry, Ivy, Nick," Cora said.

"If you don't mind, it's only been a day since..." Nick said, standing. "I'd like to be alone."

"I'll check on Uncle," Ivy said, also standing.

"Of course," Cora said, rising to her feet.

They nodded to each other, and Ivy and Nick left.

"I feel guilty for not helping them," Cora said. "But right now, I just can't."

An hour later, Cora and Brian had both changed into their swimsuits and were packing for the space station's beach. Cora stood over a bag on the coffee table in the living room, double-checking her clothes, towels, and more. The open living room sat to the right of the suite's door, with one tan sofa and two over-stuffed tan chairs surrounding the coffee table.

Brian stood over another bag resting on the dining room table, packing snacks for their swim. The open dining room sat to the left of the suite's door, with four chairs. Floral images hung around the room, softening the aesthetic.

Cora was standing in her purple swimsuit with tiny white dots when her comm bracelet chimed, and she glanced at it.

"Aunt Ferna," she said. "I wonder if I should take this now?"

"Yes, go ahead. Otherwise, she might worry about you," Brian replied.

In his blue swim shorts with matching top, Brian strolled to the sofa, waving a hand over his comm bracelet to bring up a screen. He scrolled to a show they'd started last night while he settled in.

Walking to the dining room table, Cora launched a vidchat with a floating screen as she sat down.

"Hello Aunt, is everything okay?" she asked.

"I just heard about Jessica. Are you safe?" Aunt Ferna asked. She had Cora's bronze skin and curly hair, but her hair was gray and she was heavier. "I've been so worried."

"I'm perfectly fine, Aunt," she replied. "And Brian's here, so I'm not alone."

"Well, I don't know what will happen to us," Aunt Ferna said, her face strained. "Now that Jessica's gone, we could lose all the protection for our mines, especially the more remote ones, like ours on Ganymede." Mines were the primary source of wealth for Askovs but were also frequent targets. Those without mines often resorted to stealing, so mine owners like Cora Brimble needed to pay more established owners for protection.

"Aunt, please calm yourself," Cora said. "I'm sure Jessica made plans for... I mean after she... you know."

"Nora and Eliza are trying to negotiate with Henry," Aunt Ferna said, wringing her hands now. "You know he's in charge of Spencer Industries now. I think he's a little too young, but he's the closest relative."

Nora Albright was Brian's mom, and she owned the Albright Corporation, which managed mining operations on the moons of Mars and Jupiter. Eliza was Brian's sister, in charge of Albright Mining, the family's private mines. She also ran Albright Corp, overseeing day-to-day operations.

"I'm surprised she chose her nephew, Henry," Aunt Ferna said. "I thought she vowed never to hand over the company as long as he held his dad's last name."

"Jessica said a lot of things," Aunt Ferna replied with a half-smile. "I knew she'd never follow through on that. Between Jessica and her two sisters, Henry and his sister Kaye are the most direct descendants. What concerns me is his age. I hope a more senior Spencer will help him."

"I'm sure that would've been planned either in Jessica's will or in the Spencer bylaws," Cora said. "What else has happened? What aren't you telling me?"

"Well, I told Nora and Eliza it was too soon to start pestering Henry," Aunt Ferna sighed. "They haven't even had the private funeral yet."

When most Askovs passed away, they usually had two funerals. The first was a private one for immediate family and very close friends. The second was a public funeral for everyone else. At the public funeral, the deceased's family often promoted family strength or a political ideology.

"Dear, you know sometimes I get hunches," Aunt Ferna said.

Cora nodded, remembering the years of living with her aunt, whose hunches or ideas were often correct.

"I'm having a bad feeling right now," Aunt Ferna said.

"But I'm not in danger," Cora said, leaning closer in.

"I know, dear. It doesn't concern you or Brian," Aunt Ferna said, gazing at something off-screen. "I think the general health of the Albright Corporation is at stake. I feel something very dangerous is going to happen with Jessica gone."

"Could it be you're worried about Nora or Eliza?"

"Yes, it's definitely connected to Nora, but I don't know why. Oh, sometimes I hate having these hunches."

"I'm sorry, Aunt," Cora said. "I'll keep my eyes and ears open here. Many Spencers arrived for the State of the Company address. You can keep an eye on Nora and Eliza. Maybe Brian can talk to his mom or sister."

Brian peeked at her, frowned, and went back to his show.

"Maybe we can fix whatever's about to break," Cora said.

CHAPTER 4

A few minutes after Cora and Aunt Ferna ended their conversation, her comm chimed again. She glanced at Brian and mouthed Evan's name. Brian rolled his eyes and turned back to his show. Cora pressed the button on her comm bracelet, creating a new floating window with Evan's face.

"Evan, how are you doing today?" Cora asked.

"Not as good as I'd hoped," Evan replied with a sigh. "It seems the EGS really thinks the murderer is me, Ivy, or Nick. Thankfully, right now, they believe Nick is the most likely suspect."

"I've dealt with them before," she said, frowning. "They tend to get stuck on the most obvious suspect, especially early in the investigation. Usually, they follow the evidence trail, but in this case, it doesn't make sense. There's literally no evidence showing any of you had anything to do with Jessica's death."

"They need a resolution quickly," he said with a forced laugh. "I'm sure it'll help their careers to arrest Askovians."

"Or maybe it's because this is a vacation spot," she said thoughtfully. "They can't have any bad press here."

"Yes, of course," he said. "I worry about Ivy, though."

"I wish just one time they'd be on the side of finding the truth," she said, rubbing her face. "It's so tiring dealing with the EGS and even the IPS."

The IPS, or Interplanetary Security, was an organization that acted as the police force for all humanity living away from Earth. This included the Earth's moon, Mars and its moons, and Jupiter's moons.

"I want to ask you something, and I don't want an answer right now," he said, leaning closer to the screen. Cora noted he had more white hair than red, and she wondered if it was due to stress or his age, given he was in his late sixties.

"I don't want to investigate Jessica's death," she said, crossing her arms.

"Of course, I respect that," he said, raising both hands toward her. "But if something happens to me, would you at least think about it? You've dealt with the EGS, and you know Ivy will be vulnerable. Please think about it and get back to me when it's convenient for you."

Evan's eyes darted to something off-screen before he turned back to Cora.

"Hmm... I have to go now," Evan said. "Talk to you later."

The screen went dark, and she closed the window.

Cora turned to Brian, arms folded. He closed his floating screen, ending his show, and walked toward her to take a seat.

"So, what do you want to do about Evan's request?" Brian asked.

"Absolutely nothing," Cora said firmly. "I don't want to have a confrontation with another crazy person. I just want to relax."

Brian reached for her arm with a half-smile.

"I'm happy to hear you say that," he said. "I was worried you were going to jump into another investigation, putting your life in danger."

"In the past, I've enjoyed the first steps of an investigation," she said. "But something always goes wrong." She huffed. "Somebody lies, hides something, tries to run away, and of course, there's the killing. Eventually, they try to kill me. I'm not going to do anything."

"Well, I'd rather keep you safe," he said, grasping her hand and giving it a small kiss. "I completely support your decision."

"The only thing is I would really like to help Ivy if she needs it," she said, furrowing her eyebrows.

"Hopefully, that doesn't put you in the path of the murderer."

Cora nodded.

"I like Ivy, too," he said. "I understand why you'd help her."

In the middle of their conversation, Brian's comm bracelet chimed. Cora and Brian chuckled.

"I don't think we're ever gonna make it to the beach," she said.

"It's Mom," Brian said with a heavy sigh. "I'll talk on the sofa."

He launched a vidchat, creating a floating screen that showed an image of Nora and Eliza.

"Hey Mom," Brian said.

"Jessica's dead, and we're in trouble," Nora said in a tense voice. Her son inherited her pale skin, but her eyes were green, while Brian's were his dad's blue-gray. "We need to gain immediate control of the armed guards around each of our mines. I don't think Henry Stone understands how complicated running these mines really is."

"Not even a hello?" Brian asked with a smirk.

"Be serious," Nora said, raising her voice.

"I hear what you're saying," he said, rubbing the back of his neck. "But I think your timing's off. Henry Stone is the new head of Spencer Industries, but he's just lost his aunt."

"Yeah, an aunt who never liked him," she said, her mouth set in a straight line. "She also neglected to teach him how to run Spencer Industries. Instead, she's relying on a host of cousins who don't know how to run the corporation any better than Henry."

"I'm sure everything you're saying is true," he said. "I still think it's not respectful to bother people who're grieving."

"You don't understand how precarious things are," she said. "We're vulnerable right now. If somebody wanted to take over one of our mines, there's literally nobody at Spencer Industries who could direct the armed guards."

"But for any sort of small skirmish, those guards already know what to do," he said. "If it's a larger attack with hundreds or thousands of armed guards, there's nothing Henry can do from Lunar City. We'll lose our mines."

Nora gritted her teeth and glared at her son.

"Mom, maybe we should wait until the funeral's over," Eliza spoke up for the first time. Like her brother, she'd inherited their dad's blue-gray eyes. "Brian's right. If we harass them now, we're going to make them angry. Then they won't help us, even if they can."

Nora glared at Eliza, and nobody spoke for several seconds.

"Well, let me get to the real reason I'm contacting you," Nora said. "I would like you to come back to Tymal and help us with our clients. They're very upset and worried about the future of their mines, and I don't blame them."

"Yeah, it's too bad Dad can't help us," Brian said. "He formed close relationships with many of them over the years."

Brian's dad, Benjamin, had taken an eight-month starship cruise to Mars after a fight with his wife, Nora. The ships had notoriously poor communications, so reaching him would be difficult.

"I don't think we need your dad here," Nora said, her voice edged with frustration. "If you come back to Tymal, you and Eliza can run Albright Corp."

"Maybe so," he said, his voice detached. "But right now, I'm on vacation. I don't really want to go anywhere, especially not work."

"Are you going to make me beg?" Nora asked. "I need you here tomorrow or the day after. We need you to make sure the family business keeps running. Otherwise, we'll all become destitute. Please come home and help. Come and be part of the family again."

"Okay, okay," he said with a small smile. "Let me talk this over with Cora, and I'll get back to you."

Eliza grinned, turning from her mom to Brian. A moment later, their screen went dark, and Brian closed the floating window.

Brian turned to Cora, a shadow of a smile still lingering on his lips.

"So, what do you think about their offer?" Brian asked.

"They want to bring you back into the fold," Cora said. "It sounds good."

"I know," he said, frowning. "Several months ago, when they fired me, it felt like they had pushed me out of the family. But I have a good feeling about this, and I don't know why."

Cora made her way to the sofa and curled up next to him.

"Maybe this is connected to Aunt Ferna's hunch," she said. "It could be if you don't go back, something bad really will happen."

"I don't know..." he said. "I've never been able to explain my hunches."

"A month ago, when you didn't go with your dad, I felt a little guilty."

"Why? You didn't do anything wrong."

"Well, I had the feeling you stayed for me. Nora and Eliza still treated you like an outcast, so you didn't have much to do in Tymal. That left me feeling guilty."

"These are all my decisions." He kissed her on the forehead. "I could've gone with Dad, but I wanted to build a life with you. Now, it seems they want me back."

"Does it bother you that it's because they're desperate?" she asked.

"Yes and no," he said, smiling grimly. "I know I can run Albright better than Eliza. It's just a matter of showing Mom. On the other hand, I also know I can leave whenever I want."

"Does that mean you've decided to go?" she asked.

"Yes, I'm really sorry," he said in a low voice.

Cora smiled, feeling a little relief at Brian's decision to rejoin his family.

"You don't need to apologize," she said, leaning closer to him. "I think it's the right decision for you."

"But we'll have to make up for this botched vacation," he said, snuggling with her.

"Next time, we won't tell anybody where we are." She chuckled.

"Do you want to come with me?" Brian asked, raising an eyebrow.

"Yes, but I'd better not," Cora said, frowning. "I'd feel more comfortable if the EGS's investigation was further along. I really don't trust Tate and Reed."

CHAPTER 5

The following morning, Cora stood in the launch bay of the Spencer Space Station, waving to Brian, who sat in a shuttle back to Tymal. She stood behind a floor-to-ceiling window that covered the entire wall of the waiting area. She'd shielded her mind earlier as several other people waited with her.

Watching the shuttle rise off the deck as it adjusted its localized gravity, she wrestled with an empty feeling. She wished Brian could've stayed. The shuttle made a graceful turn once it cleared the space station, heading for Earth. She watched it grow smaller in the distance, hoping she'd see him again soon. But from experience, she knew dealing with mines, their owners, and operators could end up being lengthy and complicated.

A few minutes later, Cora made her way to Evan Pendleton's suite for an appointment. As she stepped toward the door, she sensed only Evan, but this time, she braced herself for any surprise visitors. As the door slid open, she strolled into the living room and spotted an EGS agent she wasn't expecting.

"Captain Donaldson," Cora said, smiling broadly. "It's been a long time. How've you been?" Six months ago, Cora and Donaldson had worked together to find a killer. Like all EGS agents, he wore a neurowall, which was why she hadn't detected him earlier.

"Things are good," Captain Donaldson said, standing to shake her hand. He was a middle-aged man with a small paunch and black-and-gray hair. "That is, until I got a message from Mr. Pendleton."

"I didn't know you'd asked for more help," she said, turning to Evan. "It's an excellent idea."

"I thought you'd approve," Evan said with a small smile. "You've worked with the EGS before, and I know from Donaldson's reports that you two worked well together. I know the current EGS investigation is going well, but I always have a backup plan."

Cora sensed his lighter mood, though tinged with a steady stream of sadness.

"I personally think inviting me here may have been a little overkill," the captain said, frowning. "I know Agent Tate. He's a good man, and he'll follow the evidence and come to the right answer."

Cora had to force herself not to roll her eyes. She didn't feel as if Agent Tate was interested in tracking down and following the evidence. Instead, she felt he needed a quick answer, and that could be for a variety of reasons.

"There is one thing I'd like to discuss," Donaldson said. "I'm going to do my very best to investigate Jessica Spencer's death, but, Cora, please don't involve yourself. They're already upset that I'm here, and they won't appreciate any help from an amateur."

"I'm happy to stay out of it," she said, turning to Evan. "I only plan to befriend Ivy."

"Thank you for that," Evan said.

"There's another thing I'd like to discuss," the captain said, turning to Evan and Cora. "Agent Tate's investigation is focused on Nick because he was in the suite during the murder. Also, they're still keeping tabs on you and Ivy because the knife floated through the air and pierced

Jessica's heart. That's something a Mover could do."

"True," Evan said, clasping his hands over his expansive belly as he leaned back in his chair. "However, most of us need to see what we're manipulating before we set it in motion. There are some advanced Movers who could make that happen, but I'm not one of them. Of course, there's no way at this point to prove a negative."

"The last thing I want to discuss is Agent Tate," Donaldson said. "I outrank him, so I could take charge of the investigation. But I want him to feel it's his inquiry and I'll only provide support. If I need to step in and take charge, they'll be less cooperative, so be ready, both of you, for their antagonism. They could arbitrarily arrest you or detain you in a cell. They're not going to be nice about things if I need to take over."

Cora nodded, wishing she could still be on her vacation with Brian.

After lunch, Cora meandered past several hot tubs as she made her way to a lounge chair near one of the middle pools on the Pool Deck. She glanced at the shallow kids' pool on one side of the deck and noted how little noise she heard from them.

They must have high-quality sound dampers here, she thought. She removed her robe, revealing a lavender swimsuit with white polka dots.

"Cora?" Ivy called. "I didn't know you'd be here."

"Hello," Cora said with a smirk. "I'm pretty sure you've been following me."

Ivy turned pink.

"It's okay, because I wanted to get to know you better," Cora said, gesturing to the lounge chair next to hers.

Ivy removed her robe, revealing a neon-pink swimsuit. She reclined on her lounge chair and selected a fizzy raspberry drink from the meal crafter. Cora joined her on the neighboring lounge chair and selected a glass of water.

"I enjoyed your paintings at the Alinac a few months ago," Cora said. "How often do you have exhibitions?"

"Only about once a year," Ivy said. "My customers commission bespoke pieces, which take a lot of time. I put my personal pieces at the Alinac."

"Those must sell, too," Cora said with a small smile. "I had to fight off a crowd just to make it through your showing."

They chuckled.

"There weren't that many people," Ivy said with a shy smile, swallowing her drink.

"How is that?" Cora asked, pointing to the fizzy drink.

"Good," Ivy said. "Raspberry's one of my favorites. I'm sorry to change the subject, but have you heard about the EGS and Nick?"

"Yes, Evan told me," Cora said, frowning. "He only appears to be the most likely suspect. But I think this case is more complicated than that."

"He really needs your help," Ivy said in a pleading tone.

"He's safe for now," Cora said. "The EGS has no evidence. But since you've brought him up, tell me about Nick. What about him could get him in trouble?"

"Well, he's from a Viewer family, but they're poor," Ivy said. "He had to learn a skill to support himself. Originally, he was an artist, but he discovered he's a much better teacher." Viewers have the ability to see objects not illuminated by light, items at great distances, or microscopic things.

"And that's how you met him?" Cora asked.

"Yes, at the Art Institute," Ivy said, taking a sip.

"He was in his early forties and Jessica in her late fifties," Cora said. "Does Nick normally date older women?"

"Not... normally. I would say... frequently," Ivy said, her words halting. "He really doesn't discriminate by age. Instead, it's..."

"Wealth?" Cora asked, raising an eyebrow.

Ivy nodded.

"That won't look good for him," Cora said.

"Initially, I thought that, but he has no reason to get rid of a woman who's taking care of him," Ivy said and sighed. "I know his dating is... problematic. But if only you could get to know him. He's a wonderful teacher and friend."

"Has he dated anyone who's on the space station now?" Cora asked. "I mean, other than Jessica."

"Well... There's Willow, Gina, Zoe," Ivy said, ticking them off her fingers. "There are a couple of Jessica's older cousins, too."

Cora paused, taking in the information. "Do you mean Willow, Paul's daughter and Arthur's sister?" Cora asked, recalling meeting them during the solar flare.

"Yeah," Ivy said. "She was one of the few Spencers I got along with."

"Who are Gina and Zoe?" Cora asked.

"Willow and Arthur's first cousins," Ivy said. "They're almost always together. I'm surprised you didn't meet them, too, during the plasma ejection."

"What about the older cousins?" Cora asked.

"I don't know their names," Ivy said. "I could ask Nick about them."

"Yes, please let me know who else on the space station's dated him," Cora said. "Did his relationships tend to end badly, especially since he dated women who were friends or even related?"

"I never heard of anything going wrong," Ivy said, furrowing her eyebrows. "But I don't socialize with the Spencers, except for Reggie." She frowned. "That was a mistake."

Cora paused, hoping Ivy would elaborate on why Reggie was a mistake.

"I know the EGS thinks Nick was using Jessica," Ivy said, "but it wasn't like that. I think they really loved each other."

"Hmm... You've given me a lot to think about," Cora said, gazing into the distance.

Suddenly, Ivy gasped, staring at the bank of lifts. She shot to her feet, jammed her belongings into a bag, and tugged her robe around her shoulders.

"I'm sorry, I have to go," Ivy said, scampering away.

"Ivy, wait—" Cora called, peering at her retreating back. She wondered what had happened when Ivy dated Reggie.

Cora turned to the approaching man in his mid-twenties. He was an average-looking man with brown hair and brown eyes.

"Reggie," she said with a small smile. "I haven't seen you since Mabel's tea party. I met you and Ivy there."

"Yes," Reggie said, hesitating. "It's so good to see you."

She'd hoped he'd elaborate, but instead, she said, "I'm so sorry to hear about your aunt."

"Thank you," Reggie said. "Mom's really upset, and I'm trying to stay busy."

"Your mom is Teresa Spencer?" Cora asked.

"Don't let Mom hear you call her that," he said with a chuckle. "She likes Terry."

"I see," she said. "I'll keep that in mind."

"How are things going?" he asked.

"Things are well with me," Cora replied.

"Are you going to introduce us?" a tall woman with green eyes and thick brunette hair said, butting into their conversation.

"Oh yes, Zoe, this is Cora," Reggie said. "I met her at one of Aunt Mabel's many tea parties."

"Afternoon," Zoe said with a nod.

Cora nodded in response.

"This is Gina, my sister," Reggie said.

Gina, a short, plump redhead with sparkling blue eyes, nodded a greeting.

"I have to admit I find the pool a little dull today," Zoe said.

"We just got here," Reggie said, pursing his lips. "It was your idea to come here."

"Do you like gambling?" Zoe asked, ignoring Reggie.

"Not really," Cora said. "Today, I'm planning a nice, slow afternoon."

"I'd rather be doing something a bit more exciting," Zoe said, turning to Gina and Reggie. "How about another round at the casino?"

"I'm out of credits. I can't make it," Reggie said, frowning.

"Oh, you," Gina said. "Just ask Dad for more credits."

"I already did a few days ago. He's not giving me more anytime soon," Reggie said, glancing at the pool. "I think I'll stay and relax."

Gina huffed as if Reggie had done something offensive.

"I guess because we're here all the time, the pool doesn't seem so special anymore," Zoe said in a boastful voice. Glancing at Gina, they both nodded in agreement.

After a little debate between the three of them, Zoe and Gina left for the casino. Reggie stayed behind, keeping Cora company.

Later that evening, Cora and Brian had a vidchat now that he was back on Earth. Fortunately, the space station maintained the same time as Tymal. She wore her pink, fluffy pajamas, snuggled in their bed on the space station. He hadn't changed out of his business jumpsuit and sat at an office desk in his family's home.

"Well, I have a little more information on what's been going on down here," Brian said with a smirk. "Henry Stone is refusing to have anything to do with Mom and Eliza. It all started the day of Jessica's death. Mom started a vidchat with him. She demanded control of the Spencer Industries troops that protect the Albright Corporation mines. This led to a huge fight. Mom can be an aggressive negotiator, but surprisingly, Henry held his ground. Pushing back like that impressed me, and I hope I can meet him soon."

They chuckled.

"Your mom must've been beside herself," Cora said. "She can be a little short-tempered."

"A little," he repeated with a half-smile. "Sometimes she throws full temper tantrums. That's why Dad's on a cruise right now. But anyway, I don't want to get distracted. It seems the reason they called me is they needed me to open communications with Henry. I told them I wasn't going to bother him before the funeral, and Mom flew into her second rage, but I've had years of experience with that, so I promptly left the house."

"Wow, are you all right now?" Cora asked, sitting up in bed. "You know you can always stay at Brimble House if you need someplace to sleep."

"Yeah, thanks," he said, smiling warmly. "I almost called you, but it wasn't necessary. Mom and Eliza reached me with a vidchat and apologized. So now I'm allowed back in the house, and they're both tiptoeing around me. It's such a funny turn of events to go from the unwanted family member to the one whose opinion counts the most. I still haven't decided what I think about that."

"I keep thinking that if they weren't so panicked, you wouldn't be there now," she said with a small frown. "After we get past this panic period, what're they going to do? Ask you to leave again?"

"Believe me, I've had the same thoughts," he said with a huff. "But at the same time, I don't quite know how to explain it." He paused with a small smile. "I feel as if I'm where I'm supposed to be. If I don't bend and do their dirty work, I think I'll be okay, and so will Albright Corporation."

"Well, I'm learning to trust your hunches, so I'll support you in any way that I can," she said.

They said their "I love you's" and ended the vidchat.

CHAPTER 6

E van and Cora reclined on two chairs in his suite's personal observation deck, which featured a large balcony surrounded by a glass bubble, enough space for a small table and two chairs. It was the following morning, and they both gazed out at the Earth against the starry sky, lost in thought.

"Sometimes I wish I could go back in time and make different decisions," Evan said, taking a bite of his blueberry croissant. This morning, he seemed to have aged ten years, his prominent jowls and hair more gray than red.

His words drew Cora away from the view of Earth against the stars. She lowered her shield and felt his sadness, but also a healthy amount of anger. She wondered why.

"There're a lot of things I regret," Cora said, swallowing some coffee. The sweet smell of the croissant made her reconsider selecting one from the meal crafter. "But I also make an effort to refocus my mind so I don't live in the past."

They both studied the nighttime view of Earth. The splashes of city lights decorated the dark landscape, giving the impression of a slow-rotating portrait.

"Have you thought about getting involved in Jessica's investigation?" he asked.

Cora paused, rearranging her casual sage-colored dress over her knees. "Why do you need me now?" she asked, taking another sip of coffee. "You have Captain Donaldson."

"Yes, and he's going to do everything he can to find Jessica's murderer," he said. "But after Michael and Remy's murder, his investigation wouldn't have gotten nearly as far as it did if you hadn't helped." Remy was one of Evan's younger brothers, and Michael was the son of another brother who'd also passed away. "I don't want to put you in danger. I just wondered if you could strike up some conversations with the obvious suspects."

"Obvious suspects?" Cora asked, raising an eyebrow. "Who exactly are they?"

"Jessica made a lot of enemies, and she was incredibly wealthy," he said. "You could look into the angry people, the beneficiaries, and the power-hungry. Obvious, you see." He chuckled and took another bite of his croissant.

Cora stood, taking two steps to the circular hand railing before turning to face him. "But isn't that what Captain Donaldson specifically asked me not to do? He didn't want me stepping on Agent Tate's toes. It'd make him a lot less cooperative than he is right now."

"I know and I agree with you," Evan said. "If you were to investigate, say, other Movers on the station, he'd be angry. But what I'm asking you to do is have conversations with the Spencers most likely to inherit or the Spencers who are angry at something Jessica did to them." He paused, rubbing his chin. "Maybe not even a Spencer. There may be other Askovs who were angry with her."

"To tell you the truth, right now, I'm really still thinking about it," Cora said and sighed. She did her best to ignore a spike of Evan's sadness. She didn't want to launch into another investigation.

"The thing is, I can't rest knowing somebody could get away with murdering Jessica. I want to make sure I do everything I can to bring this person to justice."

"I have the impression you have someone in mind. Who do you think did it?"

"Nick, of course. Unfortunately, Ivy thinks he's innocent, and she's better at understanding people than I am."

"There's something I've always wondered about," Cora said. "Why did you let Hazel get away with murdering Remy and Michael?" Hazel was Michael's wife, and she killed them both, later escaping to Mars with her mother, Winifred.

Evan finished his croissant, placed the dish in the recycling, and stood to join her. They viewed the nearing sunrise over some of the cities.

"Remy was a leech," Evan said with a tinge of bitterness. "I tried for years to remove him from the family, but he was more devious than I could imagine."

"Care to elaborate?"

"No, I can't. I'd be violating too many confidences."

"What about Michael?"

"Michael was problematic," he said with a sigh. "I loved him like a son, but he simply wouldn't follow instructions. I blame his dad for raising him to be so stubborn."

"Are you referring to his relationship with Kaye?" she asked.

"Yes. Michael refused to leave her until I threatened to disinherit him," Evan said, rubbing his forehead. "I didn't want Michael to die, but he'd pushed Hazel too far. You and I discovered she'd killed Michael on the same day. Hazel and Winifred immediately boarded a shuttle to Lunar City and then a private cruise ship to Mars. I could've alerted the EGS or IPS, but I was torn. She'd helped me get rid of my leech of a brother, but I missed my nephew."

"Have you considered that maybe you shouldn't have forced Michael and Kaye to part?" she asked.

"Young lady, exactly how do you think Askovs maintain control?" he asked with amusement in his voice. "We make alliances, exchange fortunes, accumulate wealth needed for the next generation. It has to be this way, even if it means you lose the love of your life. Trust me, I know these things."

Cora sensed his deepening sadness, even though he maintained his smile.

What isn't he telling me? she thought. "Care to elaborate on that?" Cora asked cautiously.

Evan shook his head.

They both turned to view the sunrise. It caused the nighttime city lights to dim while daylight flooded the landscape.

Cora made her way back to her rooms and began planning another excursion at the space station. She thought about vidchatting with Aunt Ferna, who carried a lot on her shoulders, supporting Mabel.

Before she could launch the chat, her bracelet chimed. She gazed at the notification for a few seconds, a little afraid of what Evan had to say. Finally, she selected the button.

A floating screen appeared over her bracelet, and Evan's intense and panicked expression filled the screen. She had never seen him like this.

"Cora, please help me," Evan said in an urgent, tense voice. "The EGS has arrested Ivy. I don't know much, but Captain Donaldson told me they found evidence that Ivy was in the room before we walked in. He said something about her DNA and tracking history that I didn't understand."

"Wait, wait," Cora said. "Slow down. When did they arrest Ivy?"

"Thirty minutes ago, maybe an hour," he said. "I don't know."

"Poor thing must be so scared."

"Yes, and they won't let me talk to her yet," he said in a tight voice.

"What's this about her DNA?" she asked.

"I don't know that either," he said, running his hand through his hair. "There's so much going on here that I just don't understand."

"The tracking history is interesting," she said. "Because of continuous surveillance on the space station, the EGS knows where all of us are all the time. They should easily be able to prove that Ivy wasn't in Jessica's room. What's that about?"

"I don't know," Evan said in a defeated voice. "Would you please help her?"

An image of the smiling woman in a sunny yellow dress at a tea party floated through her mind. She hated to think of Ivy in the hands of somebody like Agent Tate, or even Agent Reed. Neither one of them was actually interested in finding the truth. Captain Donaldson would be open to unconventional thinking, but he needed help, too.

"Of course I'll help Ivy," Cora said as a heavy feeling settled in her chest. *How am I going to explain this to Brian?* she thought. "I'll start by trying to reach Captain Donaldson," she said.

"He's probably busy right now. They're processing Ivy, and I can't see her." He paused and manipulated something off-screen. "Based on when he messaged me, I'd say, give him two hours."

"Very well," Cora said. "I'll track him down in a couple of hours and let you know what I find out."

Evan nodded, and his screen went black. Cora closed the floating screen and exhaled.

"Might as well get this over with now," she said as she pressed the button on her comm bracelet to reach Brian.

"Hello, beautiful," Brian said with a cheery smile.

"Hi, dear," Cora said hesitantly.

"That means something's come up," he said with a half-smile.

"Yeah, the EGS has arrested Ivy," she said, frowning.

"What?" He sat up straighter in his chair. "What happened?"

"I don't know much," she said, running a hand through her hair. "There's something about more DNA evidence discovered and something about her tracking history. Evan didn't know much, and we both have to wait for Captain Donaldson to learn more."

"Oh, that's not good," he said. "The DNA will be very hard to disprove."

"I know," she said. "I need to talk to her."

"Cora, I don't like this," he said as he drew his eyebrows together. "I wish I could convince you to drop the investigation and come home."

Cora sighed, studying the pattern on the carpet.

"I know you feel you have to help Ivy," he said. "I won't press you any more."

"I'm sorry," she said.

"You don't have to apologize. Just please be careful. Someone has already committed one murder. I really wish I could be there with you, but please use the safety of the EGS. As much as you dislike them, they can keep you safe."

"I'll be careful," she said with a small smile.

Four hours later, Cora took an antigrav lift to one of the space station's lower floors used to retain troublemakers. Stepping out of the lift, she cast her eyes over the lobby with dark-gray floors and light-gray walls covered with awards for excellence.

"Coraline Brimble?" the EGS AI asked.

"Yes, I have an appointment with Captain Donaldson," Cora replied.

"Please follow the lighting in the floor to conference room eleven."

Cora turned and followed the soft, pulsating light buried just below the floor's surface. Glancing at the awards, she noted one was for gallantry. She briefly wondered what the EGS agents on the space station had done to earn these awards. A moment later, she stood at the door to a conference room, which slid open.

"Come in, Ms. Brimble," Captain Donaldson said with pursed lips. "I need to talk to you and Mr. Pendleton."

The conference room was surprisingly comfortable, with green artificial plants in the corners and a faux wood-topped table.

Cora glanced around the room and took a seat opposite the captain. A heaviness settled on her chest as she took in the captain's demeanor.

The door slid open again, and Evan lumbered into the room. He collapsed into a seat one away from Cora and nodded to her and the captain.

"Thank you both for coming here," the captain said. "This is an active investigation, and I can't tell you everything. However, our sensors found Ms. Santos' DNA near Ms. Spencer's desk and around her body."

"But the first time Ivy entered Jessica's suite was with me," Evan said in a hoarse voice.

Cora felt a pang of sympathy for Evan. She'd have to ask about his relationship with Ivy when they were alone.

"How would you know that?" Captain Donaldson asked. "She could have arrived thirty minutes earlier, killed Ms. Spencer, and returned to her suite."

"No, never," Evan said, shaking his head. "She'd never do something like that. And that contradicts the vids you showed us where we entered the suite shortly after Jessica passed."

"Based on the timing between Ms. Spencer's death and you two entering her suite, there was time," Donaldson said.

"Just a moment," Cora said, interrupting their conversation. "In the vids, Ivy is sitting on the sofa with Evan. Did you find any of her DNA there? Did you find Evan's?"

"Well, no," Donaldson said. "We didn't find Ms. Santos' DNA, but we found trace amounts of Mr. Pendleton's."

"Did you find only trace amounts of Ivy's DNA near Jessica's desk and body?" Cora asked.

"No, not exactly," the captain said. "We found typical amounts consistent with the skin cells humans normally shed if they frequent a certain area."

"That proves it couldn't be Ivy," Evan said, balling up a fist.

"Not necessarily," Donaldson said. "She could've been there several times or spent a lot of time there the morning of Ms. Spencer's death."

"Then there should be tracking data to back up what you're saying," Cora said, her eyes knitting together.

"There is tracking data showing Santos was in Spencer's suite," Donaldson said. "But the amount of time shown on the tracking data doesn't match with the quantity of DNA we discovered."

"Then she's innocent," Evan said in a raised voice.

"I'm afraid there's too much data to dismiss this," the captain said.

"We saw Jessica being stabbed," Cora said. "Why didn't we see Ivy? Most Movers need to see what they're manipulating."

"We don't have an answer for that," Donaldson said. "We're still investigating."

"So when can we see Ivy?" Evan asked, leaning forward on both elbows.

"That's the other reason I called you here," the captain said. "Agent Tate won't allow her to see anybody except her attorney."

"What?!" Evan popped to his feet.

"I'm sorry, Mr. Pendleton," Donaldson said. "The EGS is not required to allow contact with a suspect unless it's her lawyer. Please make arrangements as soon as possible. There's a lot of evidence."

"You haven't heard the end of this," Evan shouted and stormed out of the room.

Cora stared at the conference room door, wondering if she should go after him.

CHAPTER 7

Cora sat at the breakfast table, scrolling through a floating screen filled with the events lined up for the day. Her comm chimed, and she opened a new floating window to see Evan's drooping face, dark circles under his bloodshot eyes.

"You don't look good," Cora said gently. "Did you sleep last night?"

Evan shook his head and sighed.

"Did you find an attorney for Ivy?" she asked.

"Mr. Redcliffe," Evan replied, clearing his throat. "I think you know him."

"Yes, he's good," she said, recalling how he'd helped her when she was wrongfully detained a year ago.

"They still won't let me see her," he said, his eyes flashing. "I swear, I'll make that Agent Tate pay for this."

"Please don't do anything rash," she said, leaning forward. "Nothing good will come from riling up the EGS. Also, he's literally following the letter of the law."

"Harrumph…"

"When will Redcliffe be here?" she asked, trying to steer the conversation away from Evan's anger.

"Tomorrow morning," he said. "He needs a little time to prepare, and all the shuttle trips are booked for today."

"Oh, yes, of course," she said, making a mental note to talk to Aunt Ferna.

"I think I'll try to get a few hours' rest," he said, stifling a yawn.

"Is there anything I can do?" she asked quietly.

"Please find Jessica's murderer," Evan's voice caught on Jessica's name.

"I have a few plans for today," Cora said. "I'll let you know if I find anything."

The screen went dark, and Cora wondered how Ivy was holding up.

In the afternoon, Cora made her way to the center of the space station to take a lift to the spa floor. When she stepped out, she surveyed the busy walkways leading to several body care shops. A broad smile covered her face as she looked forward to getting pampered.

She walked past shops where you could get a massage, soak in a hot tub, get your hair done, and more. The reason she'd booked the appointment was because humans performed some of these services. Usually, robots styled her hair or gave her a massage. She hoped for a great experience since she'd only seen human service when she went to Rosedel, the elite district of Tymal.

After a few steps, she paused at the entrance to the hair salon. Earlier, she'd sent a quick message to Nick asking him for Jessica's regulars on the spa floor. Afterward, she'd made appointments with the hairdresser and masseuse.

"Good afternoon, Coraline Brimble," a floating robot said. It was a dusty pink and gray spherical robot floating at Cora's chest height. "Please come this way."

Cora followed as the robot glided smoothly ahead of her. They took several twists and turns along a curvy black-and-white hallway.

"Hello, Cora. My name is Aurene," the stylist said. She was a full-figured woman with curly black hair interspersed with black spikes. Her uniform was a black-and-white checkered top and solid black pants. She wore makeup that drained most of the color from her face, giving her a pasty-white appearance. "Please have a seat."

Cora grinned with anticipation. She'd never experienced professional hairstyling by a human before.

"Have you been here before?" Aurene asked, carefully separating each of Cora's curls.

"No, it's my first time on the space station," Cora said, clasping her hands and smiling gently.

"We like to offer a little touch of luxury you wouldn't get with a robot," Aurene said in a professional tone.

"What do you plan to do today?" Cora asked.

"You requested a wash and dry," Aurene said. "But I think we can offer a range of conditioners that are specifically created for curly hair. I think you'll love the results. Here, why don't you lean back and let me check your curls?"

The seat reclined further, and Cora leaned back as the chair gently massaged her back.

Several minutes passed, and she took a deep breath and sighed, the tightness in her shoulders slowly drifting away.

"I've examined your hair now," Aurene said. "I think I'd like to use this set of conditioners after we wash your hair."

A floating screen appeared over Cora's head, showing the names of three creamy conditioners.

"Will that be okay with you?" Aurene asked.

"Oh yes, I can't wait to get started," Cora replied.

"This is a hair styler," Aurene said. "It'll clean, condition, and style your hair."

How is this hair styler different from the ones I've used with robots? Cora thought.

Aurene reached behind Cora and brought forward the hair styler, which resembled a space helmet. It covered Cora's head but left her face free. The first thing she felt was water trickling onto her head, making her hair heavy. A moment later, something began to scrub her scalp, and she heard a quiet swooshing sound as the hair cleaner worked on her hair.

About thirty minutes later, Aurene removed the hair cleaner from Cora's head. Now, Cora's hair hung in damp corkscrew curls a little past her shoulders. She wasn't wet because Aurene had placed a water-absorbent cover over her shoulders, back, and chest.

"I think you should've come in earlier," Aurene said as she evaluated Cora's hair, carefully separating each curl. She frowned while shaking her head.

Cora struggled to maintain a calm expression. When she went to the robot hair salon, they almost always said the same thing before they tried to persuade her to buy something else.

"All right, the next step is to condition your hair," Aurene said. "Afterward, we'll dry it."

A new helmet landed on Cora's head. She felt the wonderful massage from earlier, but this time, a pleasant-smelling flowery substance was placed in her hair. A moment later, the helmet rinsed it off, and she heard the gentle air-drying sound that removed the water from her hair.

"And now let's take a look," Aurene said, removing the hair styler. "Much better. Now your hair's healthy."

"It's not completely dry, though," Cora said, furrowing her eyebrows.

"Yes. That's because I'm proposing a trim," Aurene said with a professional smile. "It would make your hair fuller and make the curls more defined."

"I don't want my hair cut," Cora said. She'd had this argument with robotic hairstylists hundreds of times. The shorter her hair became, the wilder her curls stood out on her head. Her longer length weighed her hair down more, making her curls appear more tame than they were.

"Are you sure? We should at least take off one or two centimeters to save your ends," Aurene said, her arms crossed.

"How many other humans do you actually work on?" Cora asked, knowing that this line of questioning would completely throw Aurene off. "I was wondering if you ever worked on Jessica Spencer."

Aurene blinked several times, lowered her crossed arms, and frowned. "I've worked on many humans," she said in a level voice. "I've never worked on Jessica Spencer. However, even if I had, I wouldn't tell you. Now, what about that trim?"

Cora immediately sensed her lie and wondered if she was trying to keep her job by not discussing clients or hiding something about the case.

"No, I'm not interested. I just wondered about Jessica," Cora asked, trying again to throw off Aurene's sales pitch.

"I don't have time to sit here and gossip with you," Aurene said. "Your hair is still damp. I can finish drying it for you if you like."

"No, it's okay," Cora said. "I never dry my hair all the way to the roots anyway. It makes the tips of my hair super dry, so I only let it air dry."

Aurene turned away, but not before Cora caught her rolling her eyes.

"Please come with me," Aurene said, while not really waiting for Cora to catch up. "I'll have you talk to the receptionist, and you can be on your way. My next customer is waiting for me."

"Thank you for your time," Cora said, mildly sarcastic.

Cora glanced at her comm bracelet. Her second massage appointment would start in a few minutes.

Cora left the hairstyling shop and crossed the busy walkway to The Massage and Spa.

She stepped through the doors, and a for-est-green-and-white robot floated toward her.

"Coraline Brimble?" the green robot asked in a cheerful voice.

"Yes, will you be doing my appointment?" Cora asked.

"My name is Holly," the robot said. "I'm your masseuse. Please follow me."

A moment later, she lay on her stomach on a cushioned table, fully clothed, while the robot floated overhead, scanning her body.

"You have a few knots in your neck and lower back," Holly said. "I'll set the massager in the table to take more time in those areas. I like to work in small increments, so we'll start with five minutes and you can tell me if you want more pressure or less."

"All right," Cora said, muffled by the table con-tours.

The massage table enveloped Cora in a soft, velvety blanket. It produced a warming sensa-tion that started from the middle of her back and radiated down toward her lower back and upward toward her neck. It was the most calm-ing, nurturing, hug-like sensation she'd felt in a long time. Then, the gentle massage began, targeting all the proper places needing muscle relief.

"And how was that pressure?" Holly asked after five minutes.

"It was perfect. Don't change a thing," Cora said, muffled by the table.

"All right, here we go," Holly said, and the sensation returned.

"So, have you been on the space station long?" Holly asked.

"No, just a few days," Cora said, fighting off sleep.

"Well, I hope you arrived after that poor woman passed away," Holly said.

The mention of Jessica's death perked Cora up.

"Unfortunately, we arrived the day before," Cora said. "Me and my boyfriend. Did you know Jessica Spencer?"

"Yes, she was one of my regulars. Coming here once or twice a week, she always requested me," Holly said, in a tone that almost sounded like she was boasting. But Cora thought that could've been a personality mod.

"Why did she always request you?" Cora asked.

"I modified the table massager so it does a test run to make sure the pressure is right," Holly said. "After that, I have a conversation with whoever needs the massage. I've discovered some humans prefer a pressure that differs from the machine's recommendations. I am the only masseuse who does that on the space station."

"The last time you spoke to Jessica, did she seem upset or angry or worried about anything?" Cora asked.

"Oh no, nothing like that," Holly said. "She was jovial, and anticipating her State of the Company address."

"Did she mention any problems with her company speech?" Cora asked, wincing when the massage went over a sore spot on her neck.

"Not exactly," Holly said. "It was more that there were some people she really didn't want to see again. Actually, I probably wasn't supposed to mention that, but it probably doesn't matter because I haven't given any names."

The personality mod probably needs some fine-tuning, Cora thought. "Did she mention anything else about these people?" she asked.

"No, nothing," Holly said. "And I'm afraid I can't continue answering any more questions about Jessica Spencer."

"Oh yes, of course," Cora said. "Sorry I asked so many questions."

"It's no problem," Holly continued in a cheery voice. "You have thirty more minutes for the massage. Would you like to discuss another topic?"

"Have you heard any gossip about the Spencer family recently?" Cora asked.

"As a matter of fact," Holly said, "there is an ongoing rift between the family members. It started about a year ago, but I don't know what it's about."

"Interesting," Cora said. "Do you know who it involves?"

"No, I don't know any of the names," Holly said. "I can't discuss specific names with you. It's against my programming."

"It's all right," Cora said. "I think I'll simply relax and enjoy the massage."

Her mind raced with a million questions about the rift.

Later that evening, Cora snuggled under her blankets in bed, this time wearing a fluffy, blue pajama set.

"Something went wrong today," Cora said, scanning Brian's face on a floating screen. "I can see it on your face."

The Earth illuminated the bedroom portal window. Even though the space station was not over Tymal, she still liked to think she was near Brian.

"I don't know what to think of Mom and Eliza," Brian said, frowning. "First, they act as if they're happy to see me, then they try to control me, and now they're pushing me aside. Today, Mom and Eliza ordered me to work exclusively with the Askov brats. You know, they're always pestering me for an early income payout."

"Is Eliza still trying to contact Henry?" she asked, raising an eyebrow.

"No, thank goodness she's smarter than Mom," he said. "But she's coming up with her own negotiation plans, and I just think that's going to be a problem." He sighed. "I think I'll be joining you in a few days."

"You're welcome anytime, but I worry about the future of Albright Corp."

"I know, me too, but I can't get them to listen to me."

"I wonder if we should start thinking about alternatives for mine management. You know, maybe some of the smaller mine owners should work with Spencer Industries directly."

"It's a good backup plan," Brian said thoughtfully. "But I think it's too early to abandon ship."

"Agreed," Cora said. "Well, the good news is no Spencer family members are doing anything until the funeral's over."

CHAPTER 8

The next day, Cora stood on the Games Deck holding a club used in the game Hammer Ball. Her club had a cylinder on one end of a tapered stick that reached Cora's waist. She glanced around the busy deck, watching others play Space Puck, Oroes, and more.

"I checked you out after we met a few days ago," Zoe said. She'd pulled her thick brunette hair into a loose ponytail, emphasizing her height and cheekbones. "You're the owner of Mystery Adventures. We've all played it several times; it's good."

"Thank you. I love hearing from the game's players," Cora said, adjusting her pink short-sleeved top and trying not to blush.

"I created my own game, but I could never get enough funding," Zoe said. "Anyway, it wasn't as much fun as a round at the casino."

Cora couldn't figure out how to reply and instead leaned over to place her yellow ball at the beginning of the Hammer Ball court.

"I've never played this game in three dimensions," Cora said, frowning. "Is there anything special about the way I hit the ball?"

"It's similar enough to regular Hammer Ball," Zoe said. "But because there are differences in gravity, it's really a three-dimensional game. As it rolls along the track, sometimes a gravity sink grabs it, and then you've lost. Other times, if you hit the sink just right, it pulls your ball forward. Sometimes it appears to go over a hill, but you can't see it since it's an area with less local gravity. The game's loads of fun."

Nick took a step closer to Zoe and wrapped a possessive arm around her waist. She beamed up at him.

Cora had shielded her mind before entering the floor and now wished she could lower it to sense Nick's emotions. I thought he said he loved Jessica.

Cora picked up her club and tapped her yellow ball, which rolled straight for a few centimeters before veering left and disappearing from the court. "Gravity sink," she muttered. She frowned while Zoe and Gina giggled.

"Don't worry about it," Nick said, dragging a hand through his wavy blond hair. He didn't exactly fit in with the others, who were in their twenties, while he was in his early forties. Stepping to the starting point with a bright-blue ball, he said, "Everybody starts that way. We've all been playing on this specific court for years now."

"Yeah, you'll get better with practice," Reggie said, taking a sip of a fizzy boysenberry drink.

Nick placed his blue ball at the start and tapped, but it went in a very different direction from Cora's. It swung near the edge of the gravity sink and shot forward through three curves on the track before coming to a stop in mid-air.

"What is that?" Cora asked with raised eyebrows. "A gravity hill?"

"Yeah, they're all over the place," Reggie said, his eyes twinkling. "Most of us can't see them, but our balls react to them. Sometimes they knock your ball out of the game, or, if you're Nick, they end up hanging your ball in mid-air."

"What do you mean most of us?" Cora asked.

"Have you heard about Ivy?" Nick asked, cutting off any chance for a response.

Cora blinked, not sure what to make of Nick's behavior.

"What's that about Ivy?" Reggie turned to Nick, furrowing his eyebrows.

"I heard the EGS arrested her," Nick said, stepping to the meal crafter and selecting a frosted pineapple drink. "Perfect." He smirked.

"I haven't heard anything," Zoe said as she wrapped an arm around Nick's torso.

What's going on with these two? Cora thought, trying hard not to stare.

"Tell me what you know, please," Reggie said as he gripped his Hammer Ball club.

"I don't know much," Cora said. "The EGS won't let anyone talk to her until her attorney arrives."

"Poor Ivy," Reggie said, frowning. "Maybe if I spoke to them, they'd at least let me chat with her."

Cora shrugged a shoulder, knowing Agent Tate wouldn't change his plans for Reggie.

"You'll be wasting your time," Nick said. "I know Agent Tate's type. He goes by the book, and he definitely won't let you in."

"Since we've established we can't help Ivy, let's keep playing," Gina said, swallowing her berry punch.

The aromas from Gina's punch wafted past Cora's nose, and she considered getting something for herself.

"You never did like her," Reggie said, glaring at his sister.

Gina blinked, and her mouth fell open

"Everybody loves little Ivy," Zoe said in a soothing voice. "Gina was only stating the obvious. We can't help her now, so we might as well continue playing."

Reggie moved to a neighboring table and settled into a chair. He brought up a private floating screen and ignored everyone else.

Zoe finished the last of her fizzy ginger and mint lemonade. She grabbed a forest-green ball and headed to the Hammer Ball court. She placed her ball at the starting point and tapped. It glided around the gravity sink, took all three turns, and rolled up an invisible hill. Knocking Nick's ball backward, Zoe's tumbled forward before coming to rest.

"You cheated," Nick said with a chuckle. "You saw the exact location of the gravity sink and hill. That's the only way you could've knocked my ball backward."

"You can see gravity?" Cora asked, raising an eyebrow. "None of the Viewers I went to school with could do that."

"Our Zoe is a powerful Viewer," Nick said, beaming at her. "Although, she's a bit competitive."

"I can't let Gina win," Zoe smirked. "She'll never let me hear the end of it."

Cora remained quiet, examining Zoe. She wondered if any other cousins were Viewers too.

"Is that a new move, Zoe?" Nick asked. "Where did you learn to do that?"

"Well, to tell the truth, I've had a lot of free time on my hands lately," Zoe said.

"Yeah, we all have," Reggie said, jumping to his feet with his eyes boring into Zoe's. "Why is that?"

"We don't need to bring this up now?" Gina said, defending Zoe. "Do you still need credits?"

"No, not credits," Reggie said. "I want something to do. Nobody at Spencer Industries will hire me."

"Well, it's probably different now," Zoe said in a level voice as her green eyes focused on Reggie. "Now that Spencer Industries has changed owners, you should probably try talking to them again."

Gina and Zoe nodded. Nick gazed at them thoughtfully but said nothing. Reggie folded his arms.

"Should I ask what happened that led to you being let go?" Cora asked, picking imaginary lint off her shirt.

"It was nothing," Reggie said, waving his hand to dismiss the topic. "I checked with the EGS, and they won't let me see her at all."

"Proving Nick was right, we have to wait," Zoe said, turning to everyone else. "Whose turn is it now?"

Gina stepped forward with a shiny, pink ball. She placed it on the start point and tapped. It followed Zoe's ball, skirting around the gravity sink and rolling through the air over an invisible hill. She shrugged her shoulders while grinning at Zoe after it passed her ball.

"My sister's a Viewer too," Reggie said. "She can see gravity and all sorts of energy waves. But you two are really cheating if you use your abilities." He frowned.

"Cora wanted to know why Reggie had so much time," Nick said, placing an arm around

Zoe's waist and turning to Reggie. "Why not tell her about the prank?"

"I don't think we need to tell this story," Zoe said and scowled.

"What do you think, Reggie? Gina?" Nick said, smirking. "Should we tell Cora about the birthday party?"

Reggie immediately packed his club and balls into a storage cabinet and stalked toward the antigrav lifts.

Gina threw her club and balls into the cabinet and shuffled after her brother.

"I'm sorry, Cora," Zoe said. "We'll continue later."

Zoe looped an arm around Nick's and sauntered away from the Hammer Ball court. She left her ball and club lying next to it.

Whatever happened at the birthday must've been bad, considering how quickly they all left, Cora thought. *Is this the rift the masseuse robot was talking about?*

Later that evening, Cora snuggled in bed and opened a floating screen to contact Brian.

She tried several times, but he didn't answer. Frowning, she studied the view in the portal, but this time, it faced a black background filled with a sea of stars.

Feeling a little lonely, she contacted somebody else. A moment later, Aunt Ferna's face filled the floating screen.

"Good evening, dear," Aunt Ferna said with a small smile.

"How've you been these past few days?" Cora asked, snuggling deeper into her blanket.

"I'm just fine, but I worry about the state of Albright," Aunt Ferna said.

"Has something happened?"

"Yes," Aunt Ferna said with a heavy sigh. "Eliza tried to contact Henry to force him to hand over control of the troops used for the Albright mines."

"Oh no," Cora said, rubbing her forehead. "Well, that explains why I couldn't reach Brian. But didn't Nora and Eliza learn the first time?"

"Wait, there's more to the story," Aunt Ferna said. "Kyle stepped in. Do you remember him? He's Jane's dad." Cora had met them both during Aria's murder investigation.

"Yes, but I think I only met him once."

"Well, he's stepped in to assist Henry with running Spencer Industries," Aunt Ferna said. "And the first thing he's done is terminate all communication with Albright Corporation."

"Oh no, that's worse," Cora said, her eyes wide.

"It was an enormous fight. Eliza accused him of going against Jessica's wishes. Kyle tried to explain he was following the company's bylaws. But Nora got involved, backed up by Eliza, and everybody shouted at the same time. Brian was present during all of that, but he wisely kept his mouth shut."

"Wow," Cora said with both eyebrows raised. "How do things stand now?"

"Nora or Eliza has turned to Brian to force him to contact Kyle," Aunt Ferna said. "Brian is resisting, which I think is very smart."

"Nora sounds unusually anxious. Is there a reason? Maybe she knows something we don't."

"I asked her that myself," Aunt Ferna said. "It's all fear. In the few days between Jessica's passing and the funeral, someone could steal an Albright mine. But Nora still should've waited until after the funeral."

"That sounds like a lot."

"Yes, it's one of those times I really wish Ben hadn't left," Aunt Ferna said, shaking her head. "Ben could've worked with Spencer Industries so much better. He's a cool, level-headed person, so everything would've ended well for us, but now I have my doubts. There's a chance that we could lose our mines."

"I know things seem dark right now," Cora said, "but I think with Brian being back in Tymal, it's not the end, at least not yet."

Chapter 9

A couple of days later, Cora took the anti-grav lift to one of the lower floors of the space station designated for EGS agents. As she stepped out of the lift, she glanced at the wall of EGS awards for excellence. *Ironic*, she thought.

She paced through the lobby, where two inebriated Askovs sat on a bench, leaning against each other as one lightly snored. On the other side, an angry woman sat with her arms crossed, staring daggers at the sleeping men. Cora briefly wondered what had happened, but she needed to maintain focus. She approached a large board with a list of about forty names.

"May I help you?" an AI attached to the large board said.

"I'm here to visit Ivy Santos," Cora said. She'd worn her business attire, which comprised a formal white blouse with a navy jacket and matching pants.

"Yes, of course," the AI said. "Please follow the lighting in the floor."

Cora turned to the left, following the soft lighting. She exited the lobby, made a sharp right, and headed straight down the hall. A moment later, she stood in front of an interview room door as it slid open. She joined Evan, Ivy, and her attorney, Mr. Redcliffe, who was a tall, attractive man dressed in an expensive gray jumpsuit.

It was the standard room with four light-gray walls and dark-gray flooring. Ivy sat next to Redcliffe and across from Evan, while Cora sat between them.

"How have you been, my girl?" Evan said, reaching across the table and holding her hand.

"I've been better," Ivy said, smiling weakly. "I can't believe they really think I'd kill Jessica. I didn't do it."

"We know all that," Evan said, patting her hand. "The first time you were ever in her suite was when we walked in together. That means somebody is trying to frame you."

"I hope that's where I can help you," Cora said with an empathetic frown. "I've been talking to other Spencer family members. So far, it's too early to say if any of them are even capable of murder." Her mouth curled into a gentle smile. "But I'll definitely let you know when I find something."

"I think it was Nick," Evan said matter-of-fact-ly.

"No—" Ivy said, but Evan held up one hand.

"I know you think he's completely innocent," Evan said. "He's your teacher, and so on. But he was the only one actually in the suite when Jessica passed away. He has to be the obvious suspect."

"Yeah, if he's not the killer, it's suspicious the murderer covered their tracks by deliberately pointing the evidence at you," Cora said. "Also, Evan has a point—it could actually be Nick."

Ivy huffed and pulled her hand out of Evan's grasp.

"I understand that you don't agree with us," Cora said. "You might actually be correct, but we have to consider all possibilities." She shift-ed her glance between Ivy, Evan, and Redcliffe. "The issue is really that Jessica had a lot of enemies, and Nick is really the obvious suspect, but he is far from the only one."

"Ms. Santos, I've read through the agent's notes already," Redcliffe said. "But can you tell us in rough terms about Agent Tate's questioning?"

"Oh, that," Ivy said, frowning. "He asked me to run through the morning. When I woke up, I couldn't find my comm bracelet. That has happened before when I've taken it off. I don't like it directly on my skin all the time, especially not when I'm painting. So I thought maybe I'd left it with my art supplies in the living room, but it wasn't there. Then I thought there was a slim chance I'd left it at the pool and I'd just get it later."

"So let me understand this," Cora said. "You routinely take off your bracelet. Have you done it around other people?"

"Well, yes," Ivy said. "I've taken it off at the pool, to paint, sometimes in class. There were always people around me."

"Okay, please continue," Cora said.

"Well, later, I changed clothes and ate breakfast," Ivy said. "Then I joined Uncle... Uncle Evan in his suite, and the two of us walked to Jessica's suite." She stopped with a shiver.

"That's okay. We saw the vids," Cora said. "At any point, did you walk toward Jessica's desk?"

"That's funny. Agent Tate asked me the same question," Ivy said. "But no, I never made it that far into the room. I basically took a couple of steps in and then Uncle helped me to the sofa. The EGS questioned me when I was there. When they were finished with us, Uncle helped me to my suite."

"Did they mention when they're going to release you?" Evan asked.

Ivy's eyes filled with tears, and she quietly wiped them.

"It seems there's new evidence that has come to light," Redcliffe said. "They found a tracking armor device in Ivy's suite. There are no fingerprints on it, so there's no way to verify that it was hers, but the EGS thinks that she wiped it clean." Tracking Armor was a tiny wire that rested over one ear. The user could prevent cams, tracers, and other devices from tracking their location. Also, the wearer could use it to disrupt facial recognition by making them unidentifiable or mimicking another's face.

"That explains why the vids didn't register the murderer in the room," Cora said.

Redcliffe and Evan nodded.

"But it does not explain why Jessica herself couldn't see the person in the room," Cora said.

"To me, that says it was a Reader or Viewer." Some Viewers can put false images in a person's mind, altering how they are understanding their surroundings.

"Not necessarily," Evan said. "Anyone with the ability to change reality for another person could have done it. For example, a Feeler could have created an emotional state so heightened that Jessica wouldn't be able to register who was in the room."

"I used to have family members that had that ability," Cora said with a smirk, thinking of her sister and cousin. "When they tried to force someone to feel something against their values, the victim became visibly disturbed. It was almost as if they were crazy. But based on the vids showing Jessica's face, I don't think it could have been a Feeler."

"Well, that was only one example," Evan said, pursing his lips. "It could also be a Reader, or any other ability."

"It's worth pondering," Cora said. "Most Spencers are actually Readers, and many of them could alter someone's ability to correctly perceive what their eyes are telling them." She leaned forward, gazing at the other three around the table. "Someone could've put thoughts in Jessica's mind so that even though her eyes saw the murderer, it wouldn't register the information."

"Have you seen the effect up close?" Redcliffe asked, leaning an elbow on the table. "Does it make the person visibly disturbed or disoriented? Is there any way to tell that somebody is being manipulated?"

"No, I've never seen it done," Evan said. "As you know, Jessica had no abilities, and neither did her sister, Mabel. I spent most of my time with those two. However, they had a third sister, Alice, who was a Reader, but I saw her very infrequently, so I don't know."

"Is there any way a Mover could've done it?" Cora asked.

"I don't see how a Mover could alter how somebody is perceiving reality," Evan said, examining something on the tabletop. "But... there are some Movers who can manipulate objects on a microscopic level. They could manipulate parts of the brain to achieve a desired result. But micro-Movers are extremely rare. I've actually only met one in my entire life, and they've passed away now."

"Could it just be another type of technology?" Redcliffe asked. "You know, like a neurowall."

"Yeah, I wondered about that too," Cora said. "Maybe at some point, a neurowall was installed in Jessica's head, and then, like in Lunar City, it dissolved so there was no trace of it. It's possible, and I've actually seen it before."

"I read about that case, which is why I brought it up," Redcliffe said. "Although, I have no idea who'd have that type of expertise."

"My problem is I know too many people who'd know how to operate a military-grade neurowall," Cora said. "And some of them are probably on the space station."

"There are so many directions to take the investigation," Ivy said, pursing her lips. "Does Mom know?"

"I contacted Leatha when they first arrested you," Evan said, reaching across the table again and patting her hand. "It would take her eight months to get here, even if she left now."

Cora wondered what Evan's relationship was to Ivy. She referred to him as 'uncle,' but Cora knew all of Evan's siblings and their children, so it must be a case of Ivy being a cousin who refers to Evan as 'uncle.'

"Well, you've brought up a good point," Cora said. "What should we do next?"

"I suggest that you keep talking to Spencer family members," Evan said. "See if anything seems suspicious or gets your attention. Anything at all."

"I'll do that and let you know what I find," Cora said.

"I'm going to talk to the older Spencers that are here," Evan said. "Also, there'll be more joining as the funeral approaches. My only concern is I've never done an investigation before, so I have no idea which questions to ask."

"I'd say rely on your intuition," Cora said. "It'll let you know when something doesn't sound right."

"I need to let you know something," Redcliffe said. "I have another very pressing case, so I need to leave today, but I'll be back in a few days. In the meantime, Ivy is not to talk to any of the agents unless I'm present. That means there'll be a minimum of a twenty-four-hour delay every time Agent Tate wants to talk to her. This is good because it'll slow them down."

Ivy sighed and squeezed her uncle's hand.

"Don't worry, Ivy. We're going to do everything we can to get you out of here," Cora said.

Later that evening, Cora and Brian finally caught up with each other.

"Evening, sweetheart," Brian said, bending to pick up a stack of folded clothes and place them in a bag. His image filled a new floating window.

"Good to see you," Cora said, wearing green, fluffy pajamas while wrapped in a warm, white blanket.

Brian told her about the huge fight he'd had with his mom and Eliza.

"I was sorry to hear about it," she said. "Aunt Ferna told me what had happened. What are you going to do?"

"I'm packing right now as I'm speaking to you," he said, with an edge in his voice. "They clearly don't respect me and only invited me down here because they thought they could force me to do what they wanted. Now I wish I'd really gone with my dad."

Cora felt her chest tighten because Brian had only stayed behind because of her. "I'm sorry things are going so badly for you," she said in a low voice.

"Oh, Cora," he said gently. "I'm sorry. I'm not blaming you. It was my decision to stay behind, not yours. What I really wish is that we could be together."

A quiet moment passed between them while Brian continued packing.

"Did you get a chance to talk to Kyle?" she asked, breaking the silence.

"Oh no. Kyle looked like a volcano ready to explode. He was that angry. I stayed quiet during the entire argument."

"I really don't understand why Nora is pushing this so hard."

"Mom said some pretty mean things. I'm pretty sure he'll never talk to her again."

"Is something happening with your mom?" she asked, furrowing her eyebrows. "Why is she so insistent on having access to the troops? Why did she fight with your dad so much before he left? I feel like there's more to this that we can't see."

"I know what you mean, and I've had the same thought more than once. I asked her directly, but she wouldn't say. Then I talked to Eliza, who also didn't know."

"Well, if you're packing, does that mean you'll be here tomorrow or the next day?" she asked, with a small smile.

"Yes, I can't wait to see you," Brian said, smiling broadly. "Then we can continue our vacation."

"I can't wait to see you." Cora grinned.

Chapter 10

Cora approached Nick from the antigrav lifts on the Games Deck. It was the following morning, and stifling a yawn, Cora checked her sage top, realizing too late it was wrinkled, but at least it complemented her tan shorts.

"I'm sorry for such an early invitation," Nick said, dusting crumbs off his black pants and white top. "I needed to meet you without 'the gang.'"

"What I don't understand is why you're spending time with 'the gang,'" Cora said, unable to stifle another yawn. She normally slept in late, especially on vacations. "You said you loved Jessica, but you and Zoe seem pretty cozy."

They'd agreed to play Space Puck, a game played on a roller-coaster-like, six-meter-long board with differing gravity points. These clearly marked gravity sinks and hills either pushed the player's puck backward or pulled it forward. It differed from Hammer Ball, which could have several twists and turns with unmarked gravity differentials.

"I'll start," Nick said, selecting five blue flat discs, or pucks. He placed one puck on the board and shoved it with his cue, a long pole with a U-shaped scoop at the end. The puck dodged past a bold, red gravity sink, moving between one and two meters on the board.

"Good shot," Cora said.

"Did you find anything when you visited the spa?" he asked.

"Not really. The masseuse robot dropped a few hints," she replied, explaining what she'd learned at the spa.

Nick nodded.

"So, what about you and Zoe?" she asked.

"I've started my own investigation," he said, turning to her with a frown. "It means I have to reconnect with Zoe, Gina, and Reggie. I thought restarting my relationship with Zoe would be the most efficient way to do that. I just can't let Jessica's killer get away with it."

"So you're just stringing Zoe along?" she asked.

"Zoe and I have been on and off for years now," Nick said with a dry chuckle. "She knows what to expect from me."

"Okay, but I've investigated murders before," she said, grimacing. "You're putting yourself in extreme danger."

Cora glanced around the deck, where only three more people were playing on the other side. She lowered her shield incrementally to sense Nick's emotions.

She selected a cup of coffee from the meal crafter while he played through his first round. His first puck got stuck between a red and orange gravity sink, but the second slid further along the board, earning him five points. He stopped and examined the board, placing the next puck, urging it further along.

"I loved Jessica, and I know she felt the same way," he said in a somber voice. "The only problem we ever had was that disastrous birthday party. We nearly broke up over it. But a lot of things changed afterward."

Cora sensed his deep sadness and despair. More importantly, he told the truth. "The robot mentioned a rift," she said. "What exactly happened at the birthday party?"

"The gang decided to prank Jessica," he said with a heavy sigh. "I wish they'd talked to me first. Jessica could be sweet and kind when things went her way, like a birthday party. But when riled, she could be venomous."

"What was the prank?" she asked, knitting her brows.

"In the gang's defense, Jessica was famous for saying she hated children," Nick said, sending his remaining three pucks down the board. The third garnered fifty points, while the remaining two got stuck at the one-meter mark.

Cora selected five green pucks and a cue.

"The gang thought it would be funny to give her an old, dirty floating stroller filled with dead plants, rocks, a filthy doll, a smelly rattle, and a moldy pacifier. Somehow, they thought she'd find this funny, given her views on children. Well, Jessica didn't take it well at all."

"That's an odd prank," she said, shaking her head. "Even if she hated children, how was that supposed to be a funny gift?"

Cora pushed her first puck down the board, and it scored ten points. She grinned.

"Good shot," he said with a small smile. "Anyway, Jessica slowly rose to her feet. I immediately began apologizing and explaining I had nothing to do with the prank. Willow and Arthur joined me, explaining they didn't know what everyone else had planned."

Cora guided her next puck on the board, and it skated at the edge of two gravity sinks that pushed it forward both times. It eventually crossed the finish line, and she won their first round.

Cora chuckled. "I haven't played this game for years."

Nick clapped.

"Play another round?" she asked.

Nick grabbed five more blue pucks. He placed one on the board and turned to Cora. "Jessica glared at everyone at the table," he said. "It felt like daggers shooting at us. Then she spun on her heel and stalked out of the room."

"Who else was there?" she asked.

"Gina, Reggie, Zoe," he said, staring up at the ceiling. "I've already mentioned Willow and Arthur, but there were all the parents. Terry, who is Gina and Reggie's mom. Lori and Walter, who are Zoe's parents, Paul, who is Willow and Arthur's dad. Then there was a whole host of uncles, distant cousins, and friends."

"Wasn't her sister there?" she asked.

"Of course," he said, taking his first shot. It cleared every brightly-colored gravity sink but stopped just before the finish line, earning two hundred points. "I should've mentioned her first. She organized the party for Jessica."

"I think you've been holding yourself back," she said, eyeing his puck with a lopsided smile.

"Sorry," he said, not meeting her eyes. "I was afraid you'd be angry if you lost."

Cora chuckled. "Who gets angry at you for winning?"

"Oh ... people," he said, placing his second puck on the board. After he gave it a hard push, it came to rest right behind his first puck.

"What changed after the birthday party?" she asked, wondering what he planned to do with all those pucks.

"She stopped all payments to me, Willow, Arthur, Reggie, Zoe, and Gina," Nick said, and sighed. "I tried to talk her out of it. Their parents would instantly become her enemies."

"She wouldn't listen?" Cora asked.

He shook his head and shoved his third puck down the board. It ended exactly behind the second puck.

"What are you doing with your pucks?" she asked, examining the board.

Nick grinned, glancing at his pucks. "Anyway, Willow and Arthur found vids of Gina, Zoe, and Reggie planning the prank. Those three had sent the vids to me, Willow, and Arthur, but I never opened my message from them, so it was Willow who let Jessica know I was also innocent. I'll always be grateful to her for that."

"So, what happened to the trio?" she asked, studying the board.

"Well, she reinstated Willow's and Arthur's incomes," he said, sending another puck down the board that lined up behind puck number three. "I told her I never wanted her credits. It made me feel bought. Also, I had my own independent income. It's small, but I can live on it."

Cora raised an eyebrow but said nothing.

"The few days we were apart, I had time to think," he said. "I wanted a relationship not based on financial support."

"Didn't the trio's parents complain?"

"Oh yes, many times," he said, examining the board. "But you know what she was like."

"A tyrant?"

"No, not quite. She could be very sweet," he said, defending Jessica. "I mean, it's true she threatened to cut off their parents' incomes if they kept complaining, but..."

Cora stared at him before changing the topic. "So, who is the focus of your investigation?"

"The trio plus their parents," Nick said with a grim smile. "I know Jessica had many enemies, but these were the most recent."

"Wait, didn't she cut off Kyle Spencer's income?" she asked.

"Yes, his entire family, actually," he said. "But when his daughter Aria passed away, she reinstated it with back pay. She also sent out a public apology to the entire Spencer clan. I tell you, she could be very sweet."

Cora resisted the urge to roll her eyes and watched him play his next puck. It rolled down the board and ended up behind puck number four.

"How are you gathering evidence?" she asked.

"I'm spending time with them, asking questions, things like that."

"If one of them is the killer, they already know you're on to them." Cora turned to face him.

"It's not one of them. I'm sure they acted together to kill Jessica."

"What makes you think so?"

Nick shrugged, placed his last puck on the board, and sent it careening down. It pushed all four pucks over the finish line, earning him over three thousand points.

Cora scowled.

Nick grinned, but when he turned toward her, his smile faded.

"Okay, I know you think they could hurt me," he said, "but the EGS is focused either on Ivy, who wasn't even at the birthday dinner, or me. The EGS is so far off the mark, and I want to redirect them by gathering some evidence."

"I agree the EGS is going down the wrong path," she said, "but it doesn't mean you should put yourself in danger. Please take the first shuttle you can off this space station and hide."

Nick chuckled.

"I'm serious," she said, frowning. She also sensed his genuine amusement and wondered how to make him see the danger.

"I know you are," he said. "But I'm not really in danger. I've known all of them since they were children. They'd never harm me."

Cora folded her arms and pursed her lips.

Later that evening, while Cora snuggled on the sofa with her white blanket and a floating screen, she tried to reach Brian, but he didn't pick up. Instead, she opened a vidchat with Aunt Ferna.

"Hello, Aunt," Cora said.

"Yesterday, I attended Jessica's private funeral," Aunt Ferna said. "Jessica never wanted one, but Mabel refused to go to the space station. She's afraid of spaceflight. Anyway, Mabel invited several close friends, including me, and we had a full service."

"Now, her body wasn't there, right?" Cora asked.

"No, her body is still on the space station," Aunt Ferna said. "So what we had was really a memorial service. However, the public funeral is coming up in a few days on the space station."

"So, when will you arrive?" Cora asked.

"In less than twenty-four hours," Aunt Ferna said. "Is it all right if I stay with you?"

"Of course," Cora said with a small smile. "Brian and I are staying in a two-bedroom suite. We didn't really need the second bedroom, but the one-bedroom suites were all taken. So, you'll have your own room, and you'll get to spend time with me."

"Good. We haven't spent much time together lately," Aunt Ferna said with a gentle smile.

"Do you know why Jessica didn't want a private funeral but only wanted a public one?" Cora asked.

"No, she never explained it," Aunt Ferna replied. "But I suspect she was afraid nobody in her family would show up for the private funeral. She wasn't very nice to them, and I know it bothered her that they disliked her so much. At the same time, she wouldn't change her behavior. She was a complicated person."

"That means in the next few days, the space station is going to become very busy," Cora said.

CHAPTER 11

L ater that night, sitting at the dining table, Cora chewed her bottom lip. She racked her brain, trying to figure out the best way to approach Ivy's attorney. Making up her mind, she contacted Mr. Redcliffe.

"Would you mind if I spoke to Ivy, but I'll only question her about Nick?" Cora asked, opting for a straightforward request.

"No, I don't want anyone questioning her when I'm not there," Redcliffe said, frowning.

"Sure, and I don't want to jeopardize Ivy's defense," Cora said, inwardly wincing. "I'm really trying to help another person—Nick Perry. He told me he's doing something very dangerous, and I'm trying to gather information to see how I can help him."

"All right, tell me about him first," Redcliffe said with a sigh.

"Nick was Ivy's teacher in art school, and he was Jessica's lover."

"Yes, I know that much. I was wondering why you want to talk to Ivy about him."

"He has started his own investigation," Cora said, leaning a little closer to the floating window. "He thinks the actual murderers are part of a group of Jessica's cousins that played a prank on her birthday nearly a year ago."

"Interesting. This might actually help Ivy's case."

"Perhaps," Cora said hesitantly. "His evidence doesn't seem very strong. I think there's a chance he's right, but if he goes around asking questions, he could be in danger. So I'm trying to learn more to make him stop."

"And how can Ivy help with that?" Redcliffe asked.

"I want to ask her about his personality. Telling him directly that he could be in danger didn't work. So, I wondered if she had ideas on how to persuade him."

Redcliffe scratched his chin while gazing at something off-screen. "This is highly irregular," he said, halting his words. "But I'm inclined to allow it only if I can get a recording of the interview session. Please let Agent Tate know that you'll be recording?"

"Of course, and I fully expect Agent Tate to be part of my conversation with Ivy," Cora said as a tightness in her chest disappeared, leaving her feeling lighter.

"Remember, you can only discuss issues related to Nick Perry," Redcliffe said.

"Thank you," Cora said with a small smile.

The screen went dark, and she closed the window.

Cora took a deep breath and grinned. Next, she contacted Captain Donaldson to request permission to speak with Ivy Santos. After explaining the issue with Nick conducting his own investigation, the captain agreed to help.

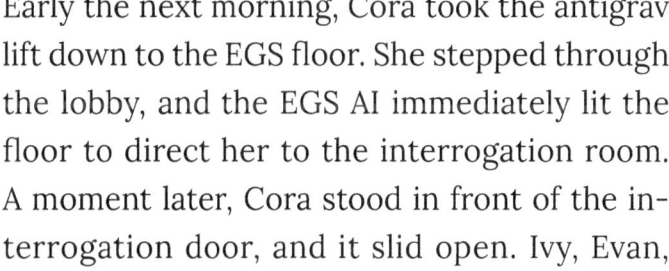

Early the next morning, Cora took the antigrav lift down to the EGS floor. She stepped through the lobby, and the EGS AI immediately lit the floor to direct her to the interrogation room. A moment later, Cora stood in front of the interrogation door, and it slid open. Ivy, Evan, Agent Tate, and Captain Donaldson sat around a cramped table with an extra chair jammed between Evan and the captain.

"Hello, everyone," Cora said and turned to Evan. "I didn't mean to disturb you. These questions are about Nick."

"I understand, but I want to know everything that happens with my Ivy," Evan said, patting the chair next to him. "Please come in and have a seat."

"Do you need to say something first, or should we get right to your questions?" Agent Tate said.

"Ivy's attorney, Mr. Redcliffe, requested a separate recording," Cora said. "Is that possible?"

"No, the only recording devices allowed here are EGS approved," Agent Tate said in a firm voice. "Do you want to cancel this questioning?"

"No, we can begin," Cora said, taking a deep breath. Why is he always so hostile?

"Let the record show that the recording of Ivy Santos has begun," Tate said, listing the people in the room. "You may begin, Ms. Brimble."

"Hi Ivy, how are you holding up?" Cora asked.

"So, so," Ivy said. "I've been better."

"Yesterday, I spent some time with Nick playing Space Puck," Cora said with a lopsided smile.

"He's a demon at that game," Ivy said, chuckling. "Have you seen the way he stacks up his pucks and sends them all over the finish line?"

"That's exactly what he did yesterday," Cora chortled.

"So, why've you asked to speak to me?"

"The problem is, Nick has decided to run his own investigation."

"He's such an idiot," Ivy said, sighing.

"What I want to do is dissuade him from continuing his investigation," Cora said. "If he's on the right track, he could be in danger."

"Well, good luck with that," Ivy said with a smirk. "He's extremely stubborn."

"I was hoping you could give me some ideas on how to change his mind," Cora said.

"I've never discovered how to do that," Ivy said, pursing her lips.

Cora frowned.

"Is that it?" Tate asked. "You called us all in for this."

"Give them a chance to speak," Captain Donaldson said in a tense voice. "I've a feeling there's more to come."

Agent Tate grumbled under his breath.

"I have another question for you," Cora said, doing her best to ignore Tate's snide remark.

"Tell me about the first time you ran into Nick here on the station. Was he with Jessica or by himself? Was he in his suite or someplace else? What happened?"

"Oh, that's easy," Ivy said. "I went with … Uncle to dinner. Afterward, Uncle went to meet someone, but I wanted to get back to my painting. So in the hallway, a few doors down from where I was staying, I accidentally ran into Nick. I was so surprised I rushed toward him and gave him a big hug. He seemed happy, but he also seemed sort of disoriented."

"Can you elaborate?"

"It's difficult to say exactly…" Ivy said as her voice trailed off. "It was as if he was waking from sleep or something. You know, the first few seconds when you open your eyes in the morning and can't tell where you are?"

"Usually when you're someplace new," Cora said, nodding.

"That's what I mean. So anyway, I asked if he was all right, but he was evasive. He kind of changed the conversation. We started talking about back in the day when he was my teacher."

"Hmm…" Cora said. "When you were there in the hallway, did anything odd happen? Anything remotely unlikely or unexplainable."

"Well," Ivy said, scratching her head, "this is going to sound weird, but it felt like something brushed my shoulder, almost like a ghost. It made me shiver." She rubbed her right shoulder. "Nick wrapped his arm around one of mine, escorting me to my suite." She gasped. "You know, this is the first time something has occurred to me. How did he know where I was staying? That was literally the first time I'd spoken to him in years."

"I wondered about that, too," Cora said. "But have you experienced that feeling before, where it felt like a ghost had touched you?"

"No, I haven't—wait a minute," Ivy said, sitting up straighter in her chair. "On the day Jessica..." She shook her head. "I was kind of crying and screaming, and Uncle comforted me. But before he reached me, I had that same sensation again. This time it made my comm bracelet fall off my wrist. It was such a strange sensation."

"Now, I want you to think about this," Cora said, narrowing her eyes. "Didn't you say you forgot your comm bracelet that morning?"

"Oh, yes. I don't know," Ivy said, pursing her lips. "Maybe I forgot I found it before I went to Jessica's suite... It was a confusing day."

"That's fine," Cora said with a small smile. "You've helped me understand something."

"I think I might be able to offer some help here," Evan said, clearing his throat. "Ivy told me about that sensation of a ghost touching her arm. It was just the air vents maintaining the room's temperature. I don't think anything mysterious happened there."

Ivy stared down at her lap and turned a little pink.

"Well, all these little clues help," Cora said with a sympathetic glance at Ivy. "Maybe it really was the air conditioning."

"Why are you asking so many questions about a ghost?" Captain Donaldson asked.

"I'm not really sure what to think at this point," Cora said, hoping that they would believe her lie. She planned to divulge her ideas to Evan and Mr. Redcliffe later, but for now, she was pretty sure about something important. "Oh, one more thing," Cora asked. "You've told me many of the Spencer cousins have Viewer relatives. Is that correct?"

"Oh yeah, actually, all of them," Ivy said, counting on her fingers. "Gina and Reggie's dad. Willow and Arthur's grandmother. Zoe's dad.

Nick comes from a Viewer family, but he has no abilities."

"All right, thank you very much for your time," Cora said. "I'm going to talk to Nick and try to get him to change his mind."

"Good luck," Ivy said, shaking her head with a half-smile.

Cora chuckled.

"Today was the best day ever," Brian said with a broad grin.

Cora and Brian were having their nighttime chat. The room's portal now faced the Earth with a tiny crescent moon in the background.

"Oh yeah? What happened today?" Cora said, chuckling. She wrapped herself in a blanket, wearing a baby-blue pajama set.

"Your aunt showed up at my house and gave my mom a total dressing down," he said. "It was glorious. You know how your aunt can be so polite and yet you still understand she's scolding you like a little child?"

"Yes, I've been on the receiving end of that more than once," she said, smiling fondly. "I usually understand later the lesson she was trying to teach me."

"Sure, it's a teaching moment when you're a child. But when you're Nora Albright, it's a war declaration." He chortled.

"So what did Aunt Ferna say?"

"She explained to Mom that by being stubborn, she's ensuring that we all lose our mines. We're going to become bankrupt because she won't bend to Henry and Kyle's authority. They literally own the troops."

"Oh, I know your mom wouldn't have liked that," she said, grimacing. "What happened next?"

"My mom gritted her teeth and glared at Aunt Ferna, who didn't back down. I think I've only seen her like that once or twice, but Aunt can be pretty scary."

Cora laughed.

"Later, we convened a meeting," he said, rubbing his hands together with glee. "It was me, Eliza, Mom, Kyle, and Henry. In front of them, we signed over management of Albright Corporation to me."

Cora let out a tiny squeal. "Congratulations. You deserve this. What are you going to do about all the whiny Askovs, though?"

"That's the best part," he said, grinning. "Eliza has to handle them."

"How did she take that?" she asked, wrinkling her forehead.

"Actually, not too bad," he said. "I had a suspicion that she found running Albright Corporation a little overwhelming. She seemed ready to hand things over. On top of that, she still runs Albright Mining, and she's doing a great job there. The real issue was Mom poking her nose into their business."

"Okay, so what happened next?" she asked, sitting a little straighter in her bed.

"Henry asked Nora and Eliza to leave," he said, beaming. "It was wonderful."

Cora grinned.

"The first order of business was figuring out when to have a meeting about our mine protection," he said, "and like I suspected all along, they didn't want to be bothered about it until after the funeral. However, Henry informed me he'd already double-checked the security for our mines and everything will continue as before until we make changes."

"I suspected that was the case," she said. "I couldn't figure out why Nora wouldn't already know that. It made me think something else was bothering her."

"I know you said that a few times, but really, I didn't see any evidence of it. It's not that she's sick. I don't even think she's missing Dad, she still goes out with her friends. Everything seems to be fine."

"Okay, I'll just drop it. I suppose you're going to have a big meeting, a State of the Company address?"

"Oh yes, and I can't wait," he said. "I'm not going to have it right away, though. For now, I'm going to send an official owner message because it feels more respectful to the Spencers."

"What was it like to work with Henry?" she asked.

"He's thoughtful," he said. "He seemed interested in my opinions, and so was Kyle. I had a very different view of Kyle after that fight with Mom. But he's calm and collected when you're not trying to make him angry."

"Well, I suppose none of us is at our best when somebody's attacking."

"All of this means I won't be joining you anytime soon," he said in a somber tone.

"It's all right, I've gathered some information about Jessica's murder," she said and explained what happened at the meeting with Ivy earlier that day.

"It seems we'll both be busy for a few days at least," Brian said as his face fell. "I miss you."

"I love you," Cora said with a small smile. "We'll see each other soon."

CHAPTER 12

Cora sat alone on the sofa in her suite after breakfast, surrounded by four floating screens. She used one to check on her software, Mystery Adventures, for any unresolved errors or complaints from her players. On another screen, she checked for any issues with her family's mine.

Suddenly, her comm bracelet chimed, and she selected the message from Nick. He was at the door to her suite. Cora's eyebrows knit as she read the message for the second time. Why didn't he just ring the doorbell?

Cora moved all four floating screens behind the sofa and stood. She straightened her soft-yellow shirt and smoothed the wrinkles out of her navy pants. Pacing to the suite's door, it slid open, and Nick appeared, but something was off.

"Would you mind if I come in?" Nick asked, glancing over one shoulder, his damp, blond hair stuck to his head as he shifted from foot to foot.

"Of course, come in." Cora stood out of the way, and he entered. But a tightness formed in her chest as his agitation rolled over her. "Nick, what's wrong? Are you sick?"

The door slid shut, and Nick stepped away from it, almost as if he expected something to attack him from there. He gestured for Cora to follow him as he stepped further into her suite toward the dining room. He paced once around the dining room table before breathing a sigh of relief. "I think whoever was following me is gone now," he said, running two hands through his damp hair.

"Who's been following you?" she asked, sensing his mind's disturbance. "I really think we should get the EGS involved. Remember, I warned you against searching for the murderer."

"I'm perfectly okay," he said, grimacing. "I'm not okay... Someone has been messing with my head."

"What do you mean?" she said, pacing to one of the dining room chairs and holding on to its back.

"I come from a Viewer family," he said. "I don't have any abilities, but my siblings do. They loved to torment me, I know exactly how that feels. Somebody has been putting false images in my head, but I can't tell who it is."

"Are you sure?" she asked as her shoulders tensed. "It could also be a Reader."

Nick nodded and pulled out one of the chairs and plopped down. After burying his face in his hands, he turned toward Cora, and she noticed the dark circles under his eyes. She grabbed a seat as well.

"I haven't been able to sleep all night," he said. "They make it worse when I'm asleep."

"Can you explain exactly what's been going on?" she said, worry etched in her voice.

"Anytime I go somewhere, I do something... I don't know how to explain it," he said. "I'll give you an example. When I walk down a hall, the hall extends forever. When I walk backward, the hall disappears, and all I see is a gigantic chasm."

"That sounds like the Readers and Viewers I went to school with," she said, scowling. "A Reader wouldn't put an image in your mind.

Instead, they'd give you the thought that there's a chasm and your mind would generate the picture."

"I hadn't considered that," he said, frowning. "It really could be more than one of them."

"So, what else have they been doing to you?"

"They started making it so I couldn't eat," he said in a tense voice. "I know I put the food in front of me, but then it'd disappear. I forced myself to reach out, and the food was there, but I couldn't see it anymore. So I basically gave up trying to eat. I couldn't sleep because I had the continuous sensation of falling, even when my eyes were open. It was like that all day yesterday and into the night."

"Are you staying in Jessica's suite?" she asked.

"Yes," he said in a quiet voice. "The EGS gave it back to me after a couple of days."

"That means a Reader or Viewer stood outside the door and manipulated your mind?"

"Not exactly," he said, shifting uncomfortably in his chair. "I've had company for the past few days." He raised both hands quickly. "But it's not what you think. The gang showed up to keep me company. Some of them spent the night."

"When you say 'the gang,' do you mean Reggie, Gina, Zoe, Willow, and Arthur?" she asked. "Is that how you know it's one or more of them?"

"Well, Willow and Arthur didn't spend the night," Nick said, in halting words. "The others stayed close for support."

"We need to go to the EGS," she said firmly.

"And then what?" he said. "I don't know who's doing this to me. The EGS isn't interested."

"Maybe, but they probably have neurowalls they can install temporarily."

Nick shook his head violently. "No way."

"I know that sounds terrible," she said in a placating voice, "but you can't defend yourself from these attacks."

"They don't want to kill me," he said with a dry laugh. "What they're trying to do is scare me."

"Why would they be trying to scare you?"

"Because I know, well, almost know, who killed Jessica."

"Okay, so who was it?"

"I can't tell you, otherwise, they'll come after you," he said, climbing to his feet and slowly trudging around the dining table. "I don't actually have a suspect completely narrowed down, but I have a pretty good idea. With a little more time to gather direct evidence, I'll know exactly who did it."

"This is precisely the time to go to the EGS," she said. "They can help you gather the last of your evidence."

"Absolutely not," he said as he stopped pacing and glared at Cora. "They think I killed Jessica. They've questioned me so many times, I understand what they really think. They're only looking for evidence to put me away. That's why I need definitive information so I can help them find the actual murderer."

"Well, can you at least give me a clue?" she asked. "Maybe I can help you and at least keep you safe."

"No, I don't want you in trouble," he said as he resumed his plodding around the dining room table. "Whoever this is, is desperate enough to kill Jessica. They may or may not kill me, but I have no way of protecting you."

Despite herself, Cora shivered at his words. She considered trying to convince him to go to the EGS again but realized he wouldn't budge.

Nick's pacing came to an abrupt stop. He peered at the ceiling, putting his hands out as if grasping at something while blinking repeatedly.

Cora jumped to her feet. "Nick, Nick, what's going on?"

Suddenly, Nick disappeared and the room transformed into a clinically white cube. A surge of fear washed over Cora and she began to tremble. She couldn't tell up from down and stamped her feet a few times to confirm she stood on a solid surface. Stretching her hands in front of her, she realized the wall was much further away than she initially thought.

A moment later, she remembered something from her school days. A set of girls had tried to bully her by using their abilities to alter her senses. They had thought it was great fun, but it could've caused serious injury.

Recalling how she'd handled her bullies, she lowered to the floor and crossed her legs. Closing her eyes, she began to focus her mind while slowly building her shield. It took longer than normal because the attacker continued to interfere with her thoughts. Eventually, she created protection for her mind and opened her eyes.

Her suite reappeared, and she peered at Nick, who stood frozen in the middle of the room. She couldn't sense his emotion any longer, and she tried to extend her shield to him. But whoever controlled him blocked her as they were very powerful.

Cora climbed to her feet and clasped his arm.

"Nick!" she said in a raised voice. "Can I help you? Tell me what to do."

"No, no, I have to wait... Just wait..." he said with shallow breaths. "They've found me. I didn't realize they were powerful enough to reach me inside of your suite." After a moment, he exhaled, opened his eyes, and she helped him into a chair. He breathed quickly for a while before turning to her. "Are you okay?" he asked in a quiet voice.

"Yes, I managed to shield myself, but it was surprisingly difficult," she said, frowning. "Should I get the medipad for you?"

He shook his head and continued to breathe hard.

Cora took the chair nearest him. "How about a glass of water or something to eat?"

"No, no, I'm fine now," he said. "What did they do to you?"

"They put me in a white box," she said with a shudder. "It was terrifying at first. But after I raised my shield, I was able to block them."

"I didn't mean to put you in danger," he said as his breaths slowed. "I thought I'd be safe here, but I can't see who's following me. Also, they've altered my mind so I won't ever see them."

"If we get access to the EGS surveillance, we can see who's following you," she said. "Reader or Viewer abilities don't affect the cams. And the EGS has the tracking armor."

"This is becoming too dangerous," he sighed. "Let's see what the EGS cams captured, and if they fall through, I've got another idea to catch them. I'm very close."

Cora sent a message to Captain Donaldson asking him to check the vid surveillance in and around her suite.

"I'll let you know what he finds," she said, turning to him with furrowed eyebrows. "I think you should stay here. You'll be safer."

"If I'd known they could track me to your suite, I would never have come here," he said, lumbering to his feet.

"I think you shouldn't go anywhere right now," she said, standing with him. "You're not well."

"I need to tell you something before I go," he said, ignoring her words. "If something happens to me, have the EGS get into my personal files and there will be all the evidence I've been gathering."

"Nick, it's a mistake for you to leave. At least wait for the EGS's response."

"No, I'm not safe here. And worse, I'm putting you in danger. I'm going back to my suite to get some sleep, assuming they'll even let me." He started toward the door, then turned to her. "One last thing. Tomorrow, I'm going for a spacewalk with 'the gang.' Before you say anything, it was planned a while ago. But I want you to join us because I don't think they'll be able to resist influencing my mind while we're all out there. I don't think they'll try to kill me or anything, but I want a witness."

"I'll be there," she said in a defeated voice.

Nick turned and left the suite. Cora stepped through the suite's doors and into the hallway, watching Nick pace down the hall. Hoping she'd see the Viewer or Reader bothering Nick, she gazed up and down the passageway, but everything seemed normal. When he rounded the corner, she reentered her suite.

Several hours later, Aunt Ferna arrived at the space station with a few of her friends who'd flown in for Jessica's funeral. Meeting her at the launch bay, Cora collected her bag and gave her a kiss on the cheek. At the same time, Ethel Meadcroft and Glenda Rowley arrived on the shuttle from Lunar City. Cora nodded to them as she had met the two women when she and Aunt Ferna visited Lunar City several months ago.

Evan also appeared at the bay, ready to meet the ladies.

"Glenda, Ethel," he said in a jovial voice, kissing them both on the cheek. "It's been far too long since I've seen you two ladies. How are you? How is my sister doing?"

"We're in good health," Glenda said with a broad smile.

"Lydia and the boys are fine," Ethel said. "We visited them for tea not so long ago."

"It's been a while since I've spent time with my sister and her brood," Evan chuckled.

"Ferna, I've seen you more recently, but it's always a pleasure to meet again." Evan leaned forward and kissed Aunt Ferna on the cheek.

"I think it's been far too long," Aunt Ferna said with a warm smile. The group turned and exited the spaceport.

"Are you part of the funeral preparations?" Cora asked Aunt Ferna.

"Yes, I'm standing in for Mabel," Aunt Ferna said with a sigh. "She was so distraught that she couldn't make it, but she's deathly afraid of flying. It's all right in one sense because she can attend the funeral via vidchat. Many of the Spencers will be attending that way."

When they reached a branch in the hallway, Evan turned in one direction with Ethel and Glenda as their suites were close to each other. Aunt Ferna and Cora continued to theirs.

"Welcome," Cora said, gesturing toward the open door as Aunt Ferna stepped in.

"Why do all these suites look exactly the same?" Aunt Ferna asked, glancing around.

"I don't know," Cora said with a chuckle. "True, it feels like being in Lunar City again." She gestured for her aunt to follow, and they stepped into the second bedroom. Cora placed Aunt Ferna's bag in the room and turned to her. "Would you like some time to freshen up, or do you want to eat right away?"

"Just a few minutes to freshen up," Aunt Ferna said. "We ate on the way up."

Cora nodded and left her bedroom.

About half an hour later, Cora and Aunt Ferna sat at the dining table having afternoon tea. Cora drank her customary coffee while Aunt Ferna drank tea, but they both selected the same teacakes layered with lemon and meringue.

"I love the smell of the lemon," Cora said, inhaling.

"It's lovely," Aunt Ferna said, taking a bite.

"I had the strangest visitor earlier this morning."

"Oh, who was it?" Aunt Ferna asked.

"Nick Perry," Cora said, furrowing her eyebrows. "He's in a lot of trouble. Something to do with a Viewer or a set of Viewers. It wasn't clear. I tried so hard to get him to the EGS, but he refused."

"I don't have many Viewer friends," Aunt Ferna said around a mouthful of food. "I don't know too much about them."

"I got to know many Viewers when I was in school," Cora said. "They can be just as dangerous as any other ability. The problem is they alter your ability to tell what's real and what's not real."

"Well then, going to the EGS won't be useful," Aunt Ferna said with a raised eyebrow.

"I know. I really wish I knew how to help him," Cora said, frowning.

Chapter 13

L ate in the morning of the next day, Cora stood in the lounge of a shuttle bay where spaceships conveyed visitors to and from the space station. Today, the bay only contained a space barge, a large floating platform surrounded by handrails. She had joined a group of tourists who were slowly suiting up to take a spacewalk.

Cora slipped on space-hardened boots and connected them to soft, white faux silk pants. The spacesuit was very similar to the one she'd worn in Lunar City, including a matching faux silk top gathered at her wrists and neck. She slipped the belt over her pants, checking its controls, when a man dressed in a green and burgundy uniform approached her.

"I'm Richards, one of the tour assistants," he said. "Do you need help putting your suit on?"

He was tall and muscular with almond-shaped eyes.

"Oh, thank you," Cora said with a small smile. "I put one on a few months ago in Lunar City, so I think I'm okay now."

He nodded and stepped away.

Cora lifted her helmet made of a transparent, soft, gauzy material and stuffed her gloves inside it, waiting until they boarded the space barge. Nick strolled to her side.

"I think Reggie's going to warn you about me," Nick said with a lopsided smile. "I just want to be clear. Everything he'll say about me is true."

"Yeah, I was afraid of that," Cora chuckled. "But Ivy told me about you a few days ago."

"Ah yes, Ivy," Nick said with a small smile. "She was the only one who rejected my advances, wouldn't even let me near her. But that's okay. I wish, when I first met the Spencer family, I'd been a more decent person. I didn't understand what real love was until I met Jessica." He sighed.

"So, why did you invite me?" she asked. "What I don't understand is what you think I can do. I don't have the power to stop an attacker."

"I know, and I don't expect you to," he said. "I hope that whoever it is will be too scared to try something in public with you here."

"Not everyone knows that I've stopped a killer before," she said, frowning.

"The gang does," he smirked, "and that's all I need." He paused and glanced at Reggie, Willow, Arthur, Zoe, and Gina. "I'm probably overreacting and nothing's going to happen, but I feel better now that you're here. Thank you so much for coming." He stepped away and struck up a conversation with one of the tour guides.

A moment later, a man in his forties with brown hair and hazel eyes stepped to the front of the group. He wore the bottom half of his spacesuit over his green and burgundy uniform. He also held a white top and cloth-like helmet in one hand.

"Quiet everyone," the man said. "My name is Jason Ellery. I'll be your tour guide today. It'll take us a little while to board because one of my assistants and I will need to check each of your spacesuits to make sure they're properly latched together. I have three assistants here, and I'll also be checking. Given that there are more than thirty of you, it'll take about twenty to thirty minutes before we leave. So, please be patient."

Cora leaned against a railing in the bay's lounge and gazed through one of the open windows at the star-filled sky.

"The sky's amazing when you're outside of the Earth's atmosphere," Reggie said with a half-smile.

"Reggie, how are you this morning?" Cora asked.

"I'm fine," Reggie said. "Have you taken a spacewalk before?"

"No. I'm looking forward to it," she said, grinning. "The last time I was out in zero gravity, I took a hike on the moon's surface."

"Oh yes, I've done that once or twice before when I lived in Lunar City," he said. "It's funny. Living there for so long, we don't do as many of the tourist attractions as we could. It all becomes commonplace."

"Commonplace?" Cora asked, chuckling. "I would have never thought of Lunar City as commonplace. But you're right. I didn't grow up there."

"So, what brings you out here today?" Reggie asked, frowning slightly.

"Nick asked me to be here," she said. "I'm a little worried about him."

"Worried about him?" he raised an eyebrow. "He's the sort of guy that leaves a trail of destruction in his wake."

"A trail of destruction? What do you mean?"

"Surely you've heard how he makes his way through all the women within a fifty-kilometer radius?"

"Yeah, Ivy mentioned it," Cora said. "But surely it's not all his fault. The women are agreeing, right?"

"I suppose so," Reggie said, sighing. "But I happen to know some of the women, and his behavior really hurt them. I think he is a sponge, soaking up everything good. But I can't get my sister or Zoe to leave him alone. The only people listening to me are Ivy and Willow. They took my advice and eventually stayed well away from him."

"Eventually? What happened?" Cora asked, an eyebrow raised.

"It's not my story to tell," he said. "Anyway, I'm warning you, too. Don't get entangled with him. He's very bad news." Stepping away from Cora, he returned to the group.

Cora turned back to the row of windows in the lounge, gazing at the stars and thinking over Reggie's words. Maybe that was the reason Nick was in trouble, but it was more complicated than that.

Finally, four lines slowly began to coalesce. One by one, each tourist stepped through a doorway while one of four people checked their spacesuit, including the helmet. Ellery checked Cora's suit and helped her attach the soft helmet and gloves.

She finally stepped onto the space barge. Following the tour guide's instructions, Cora activated her spacesuit, which hardened the pants, top, and helmet while allowing the joints, like elbows and knees, to bend. She listened for the whooshing sound of the air circulating through her spacesuit. She then tethered herself to the banister. Once everyone had boarded, another assistant came through and checked everybody's tether. Eventually, the team closed the gate on the barge.

"Attention everyone. We'll be leaving in a few seconds," Ellery said, his voice transmitting into each tourist's spacesuit. "The barge is going to take us through the bay doors. We're going to go about thirty meters from the side of the space station. At that point, we'll release the tension on your tethers and you'll float around the barge. The barge will make a slow circuit around the station."

"What happens if we get into trouble?" a tourist asked in a shaky voice. "I've never done this before."

"The assistants will keep an eye on you to make sure you don't get tangled up or anything like that," Ellery said. "Also, there are emergency robots stowed into the station's shell that will appear if somebody needs medical aid."

An alarm sounded, and a flashing red light blinked a few times before stopping. Then the bay doors opened, and Cora saw tiny wisps of crystallized air rush through. A broad smile covered her face. This was her first spacewalk, and she stifled a squeal of delight.

"The space barge is moving forward now," Ellery voiced to everyone. The barge slowly drifted upward for a few seconds and then slowly pulled forward. It drifted through the bay doors and slowed about thirty meters from the space station, then maneuvered to rotate a little faster than the station's rotation.

The entire trip around the spherical station would take about an hour. Many tourists pushed away from the barge, which resulted in many crowding a few meters above the barge.

Seeing the congestion, Cora launched herself toward the Earth. She gasped at the view. "It's amazing."

"Please direct your comments to a specific person," Ellery said with a bored voice. "Do not broadcast to the whole group."

Cora winced, realizing she hadn't set the suit's comm.

"Announce the name of who you intend to speak to first," Ellery continued. "The comm will automatically route you to the person or group you want."

"Cora, what do you think of the view?" Reggie asked.

"I think it's magnificent," she said, drifting above the barge with a big grin plastered to her face. "Where are you?"

"Below the barge," Reggie said. "Not as crowded."

"It feels so different from the spacewalks I took on the moon," she said. "The Earth's so clear from here, as if I could reach out and touch it."

"I know. Even though I've done this space-walk so many times in the past, it still takes my breath away."

She heard a tiny thunk as Reggie's voice cut out, then a new voice started.

"Hello, Cora. I hope you're not disappointed by the spacewalk," Nick said.

"Oh no, I'm having the time of my life," Cora said, chuckling. "This is absolutely amazing. I can't believe I haven't done this before."

"That's exactly how I felt the first time I did a spacewalk," Nick said, and chuckled. "We're almost a quarter of the way around the space station already. It's actually moving faster than I expected."

A tiny thunk let her know Nick's audio had cut out.

"Nick. Are you still there?" Cora asked. When he didn't reply, she gave up and turned to the other tourists, wondering if she could find Nick or Reggie. But everyone resembled each other in their white spacesuits.

Somehow, Cora floated past the mass of tourists and was now drifting outside the main group. Just as she turned her head, she saw a spacesuit drift past her as it slowly rolled on its side. She stared at it for several seconds before realizing what was wrong. The suit wasn't tethered anymore. Almost too late, she reached out in time to clamp her hands around the drifting spacesuit's boot ankle.

"Open the emergency link now," Cora said in a panicked voice. "Help! There's a person up here who's untethered."

"We know. We've sent Richards, my assistant, to you," Ellery said. "I'll be there, too. We've also called the EGS. Hang on, don't let go of that body."

"Why is he … she … untethered? I don't understand," Cora said, her voice rising.

Another hand grasped the other foot, and relief washed over her. There was a new tether in the other person's hand.

"I'm Richards," he said firmly. "Don't let go until I tether his belt."

"Yes, of course," she said, her voice shaking.

Richards wore a specialized backpack with tiny air-jets attached. They fired periodically, allowing him to maneuver along the untethered spacesuit. He attached the new tether to the suit's safety belt, and it began to retract. It gently pulled the spacesuit toward the barge. Richards followed using air-jets, just as Ellery appeared next to Cora.

"You can let go now," Ellery said in a soothing voice as he gently grasped her arm.

With trembling hands, she let go of the space-suit while Richards guided it to the barge. As the suit passed, Cora finally saw who she had grabbed.

"Nick, Nick," Cora yelled. "What happened? Are you okay?"

"Please lower your voice," Ellery said in a firm tone. "Your emergency audio is still open. We will help Mr. Perry. Are you in any trouble? Do you need medical help?"

Cora didn't answer as she floated, unable to move.

"Ms. Brimble, do you need medical attention?" Ellery asked again. "Ms. Brimble?"

"I'm—I'm fine," Cora said, stumbling out of her shock. "I just can't believe it."

"Jackson, escort Ms. Brimble back to the barge. I'll assemble everyone, and we'll return the barge back to the bay."

Turning her head, Cora noticed another assistant for the first time.

"I'm Jackson," she said in a gentle voice. "Please follow me." She extended a hand, which Cora took. On the way, Cora heard a very quiet thunk.

"This is an emergency situation," Ellery said, with an edge to his voice. "Everyone must return to the barge immediately. There is no discussion at this point. Return to the barge and we will return to the bay. The EGS is also on its way, so be prepared for questioning."

Several minutes later, everybody had piled onto the barge. Nick lay in the center, tethered to its bottom, and it slowly maneuvered back inside the bay. Cora glanced at the wide viewing windows from outside the space station. Now EGS agents framed the windows.

The bay doors closed, and the space station's AI re-pressurized the bay and activated gravity. Once she deactivated life-support on her spacesuit, it returned to its soft material. The tourists removed their suits and made their way back into the bay's lounge. The EGS agents didn't allow anyone to leave without questioning. Since Cora reached the body first, she stayed the longest.

Cora held in her tears as she tried to think of all the ways she could've prevented Nick from pursuing his investigation.

CHAPTER 14

In the middle of the afternoon the next day, Cora entered the EGS conference room. Ivy, Evan, and Captain Donaldson sat around a large oval table. As Cora took her seat, she nodded to Mr. Redcliffe, who'd called the meeting. Cora noted they were in a much more comfortable room, complete with a meal crafter and drinks for everyone present. She thought it must be the influence of Ivy's attorney.

"Based on our current evidence, I think the EGS should release Ivy Santos," Mr. Redcliffe said, his voice stern.

"That won't happen," Captain Donaldson said. "Even though we've had another death, the evidence for the first murder points to Ms. Santos."

"But that's not fair," Evan said, flexing a fist. "There's no way she could have killed Jessica and Nick."

"Mr. Pendleton, we have to follow the evidence," the captain said. "So far, her DNA, comm data, and tracking armor all put her in the suite when Ms. Spencer was murdered."

"You're not suggesting a second murderer attacked Mr. Perry?" Redcliffe asked. "The fact that someone murdered Perry and Spencer, the occupants of the same room, points to one killer."

"Just because we're not releasing Ms. Santos doesn't mean we're not examining more evidence," Donaldson said. "Even now, Agent Tate is examining Mr. Perry's crime scene."

"What have you found?" Cora asked, hesitantly.

"Agent Tate and I have agreed to show you the surveillance vids," the captain said. "Cora, since you were there, we'd like your input. Let us know if we missed something." He turned to Ivy. "Would you let us know if you see something unusual? He toured with a number of friends you already know."

Ivy nodded.

Donaldson pressed a button on the conference room table, creating a floating screen positioned at the end of the table.

"First, observe the floating barge," the captain said. "Some of the tourists have already floated off, and that includes Nick Perry. For a couple of seconds, the AI highlights Nick in a pink glow. Now notice how he floats out of view of the first cam."

"Why don't you have continuous coverage of the outside of the space station?" Cora asked. "Are some broken, or is that a security design?"

"It was the original surveillance design. I never understood why it wasn't updated."

"So somebody who's spent a lot of time on the space station may have found the blind spots between the cams," Evan said.

"Yes, Tate and I discussed that," Donaldson said. "A few minutes later, notice that Mr. Perry floats in view of the next cam. The AI highlights Nick again in pink. You can see on the vid he is moving and active. But he taps his belt a few times. We think he was trying to restart the spacesuit's respirator."

"I didn't even know you could restart the respirator there," Cora said. "I think that's important because most tourists wouldn't know that. It means Nick had also been outside many times and knew a lot about spacesuits."

Donaldson nodded.

"All right, note the frequency of his tapping starts to increase. But then he eventually drifts out of view of this cam."

Evan grunted with a sour face.

"I want to pause here for a minute," Donaldson said. "Mr. Perry is drifting at the same rate. In the vids, nothing or no one has impacted him to cause him to change direction. The only thing we see him do is push a button on his belt." He paused and gazed at everyone in the room. "He should have appeared in front of the third cam, but he never did. I'll fast-forward a few minutes through the third cam's vid."

"Some tourists did float in view of the third cam," Cora said.

"Yes, Tate interviewed all five of them, but they never saw anything," the captain said. "People never see anything…" He grumbled under his breath.

"The next thing that happened was Mr. Perry floated into view of cam number ten," Donaldson said. "It's used for longer distances. Watch as Ms. Brimble catches one leg."

Cora shivered as if she were re-living finding Nick dead. Evan grasped her hand and gave her a warm smile.

"I didn't know it was Nick at that time," Cora said, her voice very solemn. "If I'd realized he was in trouble, maybe I could've…"

"There was nothing you could do," Evan said, patting her hand.

"Mr. Pendleton is right," Captain Donaldson said. "But you helped us, anyway. Tate used your and Richards' testimony to fill in what happened."

Cora watched as Richards rescued Nick, and Jackson guided her to safety. A new vid showed all four of them landing on the open barge.

"So, it's fairly clear to me that the attack happened somewhere between the second and third cams' field of view," Donaldson said.

"Who were the five tourists that drifted into view of the third cam?" Cora asked. "Ms. Jackson, the assistant who accompanied you. Ms. Gina and Zoe Spencer. Mr. Reggie and Arthur Spencer."

"What happened to Willow Spencer?" Cora asked.

"She didn't show in the vids," the captain said with knit eyebrows. "Is that important?"

"Not sure…" Cora's voice trailed away. "It's just that she's normally part of that group."

"Given that something happened to damage Mr. Perry's spacesuit, do we know how it was done?" Mr. Redcliffe asked.

"Have you seen this?" Donaldson asked. He laid a dull, metal instrument on the table, which curved a little like a snake and contained various hooks sticking out at odd angles.

"Have you seen that before, Ivy?" Redcliffe asked.

She shook her head, her eyes wide.

"This is used to install respirators, which recycle breathable air in the spacesuit before passing it to the breather," the captain said. "One is missing from the tour guide's maintenance locker. Our theory is one of these was used on Mr. Perry's respirator, causing it to malfunction. He wouldn't have realized it had malfunctioned until he was already outside, because of the reserve air in the suit. Also, if the respirator had been disabled before the tour guide's checks, they would've caught it."

"Someone sabotaged his suit during the spacewalk?" Cora asked with raised eyebrows. "That's very bold. Or the act of somebody desperate."

"There's a chance this could be a simple accident," Donaldson said unconvincingly. "Agent Reed has been looking into that."

"It's very unlikely that the respirator worked perfectly before exiting the bay and then suddenly stopped working," Mr. Redcliffe said.

"True. They all go through a diagnostic check before every trip," Donaldson said. "It's never had problems before."

"Did you find any other evidence, like DNA, for example?" Mr. Redcliffe asked.

"Yes," Donaldson said. "There is some residual DNA on the respirator tool we found on the inside of his belt. But nothing unusual. Most of it was actually Mr. Perry's."

"I need to add a few more things," Cora said and paused for a moment to gather her thoughts. "Captain Donaldson, did you get the message to check the surveillance around my suite a couple of days ago?"

"Yes, I received it," the captain said. "I have to admit, I didn't really check anything until today. The only person in the hallway was Nick Perry."

"That means someone powerful enough to manipulate minds at great distances is behind this," Cora said, shaking her head. "I mentioned earlier that Nick was doing his own investigation. He figured out who the murderer was, and I think he somehow alerted them. Now, before he passed away, Nick told me that he had secret files that revealed the name, or names, of the murderer. And he asked me to make sure to tell the EGS."

"Did he say where these files were?" Donaldson asked.

"No, he wouldn't," Cora said. "He repeated that the EGS could find them. He was trying not to think about them so that whoever was attacking him wouldn't find the files first."

"What do you mean by 'attacking him'?" Ivy asked.

"He felt that a Viewer was putting images in his mind," Cora said. "And as you know, he couldn't defend himself, as he had no abilities. But it could've also been a Reader."

"But there are so many Readers and Viewers here," Ivy said, her tone darkening. "There'd be no way to narrow down who could've attacked him or why."

"Exactly. He was really struggling," Cora said.

"Poor Nick," Ivy said, wiping her eyes.

Evan exhaled, leaning back in his chair. "This is more complicated than I originally suspected."

"I don't want you involved in this case," the captain said, turning to Cora. "But I know from experience you'll do whatever you want. Please contact me on my private comm no matter the time. I don't want to investigate a third murder."

She nodded, knowing she couldn't let a murderer run free on the space station.

CHAPTER 15

The following afternoon, Cora made it to the space station's beach. She stepped out of the antigrav lift and gasped with wide eyes. A large sandy beach, interspersed with palm trees, faced an enormous ocean that appeared to extend over the horizon. It was a blend of a hologram with a sandy beach and saltwater.

"Who in the world thought putting an entire beach in space was a good idea?" she said as a slow grin covered her face. "Beautiful." She stood for a moment as the salty air wafted over her and the sun's rays warmed her body.

"Cora, over here!" Evan called. He reclined on a lounge chair in a casual, blue-and-white-striped top and dark-blue shorts. Cora had never seen him dressed so informally. She stifled a giggle as he lay back sipping a cocktail at the beach. It seemed like such a cliché.

Cora slipped off her shoes and let her toes sink into the sand with each step. She wore a peach top with teal-green shorts as she made her way over the warm sand. The sound of the ocean must have been augmented with audio, as it sounded like an ocean on Earth instead of the large floor of a space station. But the hologram created warm sunlight from a setting sun and palm trees leaning over the sand, which enhanced the feeling of really being on a beach.

"That drink looks good. What are you having?" Cora asked as she took the second lounge chair on the other side of a small table, which featured a meal crafter.

"I don't remember the name, but it's something frosty with strawberries. I can order it for you if you like," Evan said with a half-smile.

"No, it's okay. I've just had coffee. I think what I'd really like is water," Cora said as she scrolled through the menu on the crafter and selected a glass of ice-cold water.

Cora glanced around the beach, searching for anybody else who might be enjoying it with them.

"No, there's nobody else here," he said with a grin. "Being a Pendleton has its privileges." He raised an eyebrow and swallowed more of his strawberry frosty.

Cora took the opportunity to gradually lower her shield. She did it in small increments because even though Evan appeared jovial, he was actually broadcasting huge waves of deep despair. Cora wondered if she should talk to him about his sadness but decided to let him lead the conversation.

"I suppose you're wondering why I asked you here," he said, gazing out over the expansive ocean.

"I suppose that you wanted to discuss Ivy's defense," she said, inhaling the warm air. "But right now, I don't have any ideas."

"That and everything else," he said with a heavy sigh. "Cora, I feel like such a failure. I've let Ivy down. I let Jessica down, and I feel as if everything I try just isn't working."

"But you're doing your level best," she said with a concerned expression. "You've hired people you thought were the best to help Ivy. Also, I'm not sure you could have done anything to help Jessica. That doesn't make you a failure."

Evan didn't immediately reply but stared out at the water for a moment.

"There's something I want to tell you," he said eventually. "Something about me and Jessica."

Cora waited, unsure if he expected her to say something. When another minute passed, she turned to him. "What is it you wanted to tell me?" she asked in a gentle voice.

"Many, many years ago, Jessica and I were married," Evan said, lowering his voice.

Cora stifled her gasp, but she remembered Aunt Ferna referring to something about a tragic event between Evan and Jessica.

"We even had a daughter. Her name was Una." His face changed to a very sad smile.

"Una's a beautiful name. Was the problem that your parents didn't approve of your match?"

"Yes, absolutely." He chuckled. "My father hated Jessica's dad. Our fathers had an extreme rivalry, and us getting married was the ultimate insult to both sides. Then, worse, for them, we had a daughter, and they were beside themselves. You see, my mother and aunts all doted on Una, and the same with the Spencer side. Jessica's mom, sisters, and aunts loved Una. The only people having a problem with us were our fathers."

"Well, I remember Hazel having an issue with the support the Pendletons gave Kaye instead of her. Hazel was his legal wife, and Kaye his girlfriend."

"Yes, I know," he said, exasperation in his voice. "Ironic. Years later, I stood in my father's place, opposing a relationship between two people who genuinely loved each other—Michael and Kaye. But all I can say is now I have a much better understanding of why my father opposed our relationship so much."

"Are you going to talk about family obligations, the power structure, and maintaining our place in society?" she asked with a sarcastic smirk.

"Yes, that's exactly right," he said with a sigh. "You're young, and you don't understand. Jessica and I railed against our fathers, and it was almost workable. Michael and Kaye railed against me, and I would have given in, except I had already made a deal for him to marry."

"Why did you agree to Hazel and Michael's marriage?"

"We needed the credits. I know our family has many Askovians, and we wield a lot of political influence. But there are a lot of mouths to feed, and quite frankly, many times we simply need the credits."

Cora was silent for a while as she reflected on the trouble Hazel encountered in the Pendleton family.

"The bickering between our families eventually broke us up," Evan said. "So that meant that Una had to be flown between our two homes, and that's where the problem started."

"That must've been hard on your daughter."

"The separation caused unbelievable tension in both families. Then she died in a hovercar accident."

"Oh, I'm so sorry to hear that," she said, now understanding some of the depth of his feelings. It wasn't just that Jessica died, it was that Jessica was the last of the little family they'd created many years ago.

"Yes, it was a mess," he said. "Jessica blamed me because I was supposed to escort Una back to the Spencers' home. I blamed Jessica even though I was angry at our fathers."

"So that's why you were initially lenient about Michael and Kaye," she said, leaning on an elbow toward him.

"Yes, it was a mistake. As soon as he married Hazel, I should have forced him to end his relationship with Kaye. But I kept remembering my relationship with Jessica and how much I despised my father for breaking us up."

Cora studied his projected emotions for a moment, amazed that he never considered his behavior as wrong.

"Earlier you asked a question. 'Why did Jessica invite me and Ivy to her suite?'" Evan said. "Ivy is my daughter. Years after Una passed away, I married Leatha, a Viewer who's actually related to the Spencer family, ironically. Ivy knows I'm her dad, and I've been in her life since she was born. But I've worked very hard to keep her hidden from Jessica. In public, I've asked Ivy not to refer to me as dad for her own safety. It's actually been fairly easy because Ivy and I usually don't socialize in public together. But Jessica found out anyway."

"I suppose that must have been Remy?" she asked with a raised eyebrow.

"Yes, you've guessed it," he said in a tense voice. "Remy was a blackmailer and never missed an opportunity to make my life miserable. When I refused to pay, he ran to Jessica. I know he was expecting a huge fallout, but instead, Jessica surprised all of us. She sent a wonderful message welcoming Ivy to her family. Like I said, I married into a family branch of the Spencers, and Ivy is some sort of distant cousin. She then requested that we visit, but my schedule wouldn't permit for a while. Then we settled on a meeting at the space station where she was giving the State of the Company address. There would be many other relatives here that Ivy would get to know."

"This should have been a happy reunion," Cora said with a sigh. "I'll do everything I can to find out what happened to Jessica and Nick."

CHAPTER 16

The next day, Cora attended Jessica Spencer's funeral, held on the observation deck. She took in the stars in the sky and the lighted cities experiencing night on Earth, even though it was afternoon on the space station. The officiant for the funeral was an older woman who had known Jessica since she was a little girl.

"Hello everyone. I'm Delphine," she said in a somber tone. Her shoulder-length gray hair brushed over her shoulders as she nervously smoothed out a dark-green dress. "As you all know, this funeral is a little irregular, but Jessica didn't want a private funeral. She always knew what she wanted and wasn't afraid to go after it. Many years ago, Jessica asked me to speak at her funeral if she passed before me. I really never thought this day would come." She paused for several seconds, blinking back tears before continuing.

"Poor Delphi," Aunt Ferna whispered as she wiped away a stray tear.

Cora reached for her aunt's hand and gave it a gentle squeeze.

"I've known Jessica since she was a little girl," Delphine said in a wobbly voice. "Over the decades, I've had the privilege of seeing that sweet and kind little girl transform into a powerful leader of the largest and most influential mining corporation."

Cora did her best to pay attention, but after Delphine continued for a few more sentences, her mind wandered off. She glanced at the second row, which included the Spencers who had been with Nick a few days ago. She expected Gina, Reggie, Willow, and Zoe to be sitting with their parents, but their parents sat in the front row, and they sat behind. Her mind dwelled on that for a moment before drifting to other topics.

Cora sighed, and Aunt Ferna reached for her hand and gave it a few pats.

"Don't worry, it won't last too much longer," Aunt Ferna said, like she was encouraging a little child.

Cora stifled a giggle.

An hour later, after almost every Spencer family member stood up to proclaim Jessica's greatness, the official portion of the funeral ended. During the speeches, Cora had to stop herself many times from rolling her eyes. Knowing the strife Jessica caused among her family members and business partners, Cora wondered how they could all say such wonderful words about her.

Aunt Ferna nudged her, breaking her out of her reverie. Cora stood and followed the crowd to a separate reception area still on the observation deck. The crowd shuffled past the anti-grav lifts to the other side of the deck, where several tables and chairs were arranged for the attendees.

Several minutes later, Cora sat across from Aunt Ferna, taking a bite of a mini cheese quiche.

"It's all right, but a little dry," Aunt Ferna said.

Willow and Arthur's dad, Paul, sat next to Aunt Ferna. He looked like an older version of his son with the same blue-green eyes, except he was graying at the temples. Cora had met them briefly in Lunar City, but now she had more time to actually talk to them.

"So, have you heard about the fight between Kyle, Henry, and the Albright Corporation?" Paul said, shaking his head.

"Oh yes, we're very familiar with that," Aunt Ferna said in a firm voice. "I had to sit Nora down and have a strong discussion with her to make her stop badgering Henry and Kyle. I know things are going well now."

"Oh, I didn't know that," Paul said, raising one eyebrow. "Kyle and Henry don't talk to the rest of us too much, but I always try to be kind to them."

"I hope you don't think I'm prying, but why don't they speak to you?" Cora asked.

"Oh, because of Jessica," Paul said with a sigh. "Jessica hated both Henry and Kyle, but for different reasons. Henry had the audacity to be born into the Stone family, and his parents decided to give him their last name. Kyle was dumb enough to recommend a good solution to a problem we were having on one of Mars' moons. Jessica almost attacked Kyle when she discovered the solution would also help Pendleton Mining."

"Jessica's hatred for Evan was sometimes pathological," Aunt Ferna said with a sad face. "I understood why she didn't like him, but really, it caused so many problems."

Cora maintained her silence, pondering his words.

"We initially fell out of favor after my children decided to play a nasty prank on Jessica," Paul said, pursing his lips. "We eventually got that resolved. Willow and Arthur didn't understand what the prank was. Jessica decided not to hate them, but it caused all sorts of tension within the family members."

"Yes, she had a way of separating people who would normally have gotten along," Aunt Ferna said.

"Can you tell me something more about the prank?" Cora asked, relieved someone else brought up the topic.

"Well, first of all, it wasn't Willow and Arthur's decision," Paul said, as his eyebrows knit. "It was Gina and Reggie. They're always up to something. Though don't let me forget Zoe. So, if there's something mischievous to be done, those three will find it." He grumbled. "They delivered some hideous baby carrier. It reminded Jessica of her lost child. But the problem was, Willow and Arthur never knew that was the prank. It was something the other three cooked up and then, at the last minute, asked my kids to join in. The only thing that saved them is they immediately apologized, basically groveled, because they didn't want to hurt Jessica's feelings."

"I remember Jessica's face," Aunt Ferna said in a quiet voice. "She looked... I don't know how to describe it... hurt? No, destroyed. As if she couldn't believe somebody would make fun of the death of her child. That's one of the few times I've felt very sorry for Jessica."

Hearing this side of the prank caused Cora to understand how deeply Jessica had been hurt. Jessica was the sort of person who never showed emotions in public, except anger, of course. Aunt Ferna's description of her pain made her understand its depth.

"That must have cut deep," Cora said.

"Oh yes, I was there, too," Paul said, frowning. "If I didn't think Jessica would fire a blaster at me, I would've gone and hugged her. But actually, my children apologizing profusely seemed to make a difference. She simply left the room."

"This is all your fault!" A loud female voice floated toward their table.

Paul jumped to his feet, racing toward the commotion. Cora stood as she could see a physical scuffle but couldn't tell exactly what was happening.

"You've made us all poor now!" another female voice shouted.

"I didn't do anything!" a new female voice chimed in.

The entire room grew quiet, and everyone turned to watch the commotion, stepping away from the fight. Now Cora could see a physical altercation between Zoe, Gina, and Willow. In the middle was Reggie, trying to reason with Gina while Arthur pushed Zoe away from Willow. This caused Zoe's dad, Walter, to appear between Zoe and Arthur.

Walter yelled at Arthur with his tall, imposing frame. "Get your hands off my daughter." He had the same thick, brown hair as his daughter. "If you ever touch her again, I'll kill you."

"Now dear, calm down. Let's go." Lori, Zoe's mom, shared the same green eyes as her daughter. "Come along, come along." She pulled on her daughter's arm while gently nudging her husband to the lifts. Eventually, the two relented and followed Lori off the observation deck. Zoe exchanged a couple of shouts with Gina and Willow. A few minutes later, they entered the lift.

The silence that had descended earlier erupt-ed into intense whispers. Paul stood between Arthur and Willow, who wept on his shoulders. He talked quietly with Arthur before leading them to the lifts.

"Goodness, what was that about?" Cora asked, peering at Gina, who stood in the middle of the floor with her arms crossed. Gina was having a defiant conversation with her mom, Terry, who had the same red hair and blue eyes as her daughter. Everyone still gave them a lot of space while pretending not to eavesdrop on their conversation.

"I don't know," Aunt Ferna said. "Hopefully, it's over."

Reggie ran a hand through his hair, said some-thing into his mom's ear, and left the reception room. After a while, Gina's mom coaxed her to a deserted table where they continued their discussion.

The rest of the reception went with no more interruptions. While Cora had a cup of coffee and Aunt Ferna some tea, they both ate a sum-mer blueberry layered tart, which turned out to be in Jessica's honor. The smell of the blueber-ries filled her nostrils and reminded her of many of the tea parties she'd had at Mabel's as a child. It brought a sad smile to her face.

Much later that evening, Cora sat in the dining room of her suite. Aunt Ferna had gone to bed an hour earlier, and she should have done the same. But Brian wasn't available this evening. Sipping on a glass of water, she wondered what to do about her investigation into Nick's death. She just couldn't let someone get away with taking his life.

She jumped when her comm bracelet chimed, noticing the late hour of the vidchat.

"I hope I didn't wake you," Captain Donaldson said. He had large circles under his eyes.

"Oh, that's all right," Cora said. "I was at Jessica's funeral and then later the reception. So, I was having trouble falling asleep."

"Well, I'll make this quick," the captain said. "We finally located Nick's private files, and now I see why he never told you where they were. They were very easy to find."

"I feel like I'm hearing a 'but,'" Cora said hesitantly.

"Yes," Donaldson said. "Whoever found them first removed all the contents but left the files there. It was as if they were taunting us."

"Yeah, I had a bad feeling about that," Cora said. "When he wouldn't say where the files were, he assumed it would be easy for you to find. But that meant it would be easy for the killer to find them, too." She sighed. "So there's still no additional progress?"

"We've made some progress, but I'm not at liberty to say at the moment," Donaldson said. "Agent Tate might have more questions for you. You're not planning to leave anytime soon, right?"

"No, not at all. The attorneys should execute Jessica's will soon," Cora said, sighing. "I know I'm not in the will, but there is a small chance Aunt Ferna might be."

"Oh, I see. Well, let me know if you hear of anything interesting."

As the floating screen went dark, Cora wondered what Jessica's will would reveal.

CHAPTER 17

C ora and Aunt Ferna stood outside of the door to Evan's suite. Aunt Ferna had asked the AI to alert Evan they were there, but several seconds had gone by. Cora felt Evan's deep despair and began to understand why her aunt insisted on meeting him right away.

"I wish you'd tell me what this is all about," Cora said, adjusting her yellow shorts and straightening her white top, wishing she'd dressed a bit more formally.

"Trust me, dear," Aunt Ferna replied, wearing one of her flowery afternoon tea dresses. "This is important, and we may even save a life." She turned to the door. "Alert Evan Pendleton that we're waiting for him."

One of Aunt's hunches? Cora thought.

A moment later, the door slid open, and Evan appeared in the doorway. His eyes were red as if he'd been crying, and his formal jumpsuit was rumpled as if he'd slept in it.

Evan's deepening ache of misery, guilt, and regret hit Cora in crashing waves. She immediately raised her mental shield and nearly sighed with relief.

"Ferna, I'm sorry," Evan said, his voice croaky. "This is not a good time for me."

Aunt Ferna gently grasped his right arm and guided him to the sofa. Cora followed, her eyebrows raised, wondering what her aunt could be up to. She sat on a chair opposite them as Aunt Ferna and Evan sat together. She patted his hand.

"I know the Spencers' attorney has sent out the portions of the will relevant to each of us," Aunt Ferna said gently. "I was worried something in the will might upset you. This is not the time for you to grieve alone."

An errant tear escaped Evan's eyes, and he quickly wiped it away, taking a deep breath.

"You're right," Evan said, clearing his throat. "I got official notification from the attorney yesterday during the reception. I didn't see it because I was with Ivy and Redcliffe. It was a personal message addressed to me." He glanced at Aunt Ferna and Cora. "Now, if you don't mind, I'd like to be alone."

"Maybe it's time to get your wife here," Aunt Ferna suggested. "After all, she must be worried sick about Ivy."

"Leatha's visiting family in Anteros," he said. "It would take her eight months to get here. Anyway, I promised her I'd keep Ivy safe."

"I know you're used to handling everything, but this is different," Aunt Ferna insisted. "You need support, too."

"I'm fine," he said, shaking his head.

"Do you want to talk about it?" Aunt Ferna asked in her calm voice.

"I'd forgotten how pushy you could be," Evan chuckled.

"It's not pushy, exactly," Aunt Ferna replied with a lopsided smile. "I think of it as helping. Sometimes people don't know when they really need help."

Cora and Evan chuckled. Aunt Ferna had a way of 'encouraging' loved ones, even against their wills.

"There, you look better already," Aunt Ferna said. "Now tell me, what have you had for breakfast this morning?"

"Oh, I haven't eaten yet," he admitted. "I fell asleep on the sofa late last night rereading Jessica's message."

"If you like, I can select eggs and synthetic sausage, or a blueberry scone?" Cora offered.

"I think both of you are kind of pushy," Evan said with a small smile. "I'd just like a cup of coffee."

Cora selected the coffee and a blueberry scone from the meal crafter. It materialized on the table closest to Evan. He swallowed half a cup of coffee and exhaled, his face relaxing almost back to normal. He broke off a piece of the scone and chewed on it for a moment.

"Well, I don't mind telling you some of the contents of her message," he said. "Essentially, Jessica changed her will after her last birthday party. Her personal fortune was several hundred million credits. Originally, she was going to divide it evenly between her niece, nephew, and younger cousins. There are twelve in total, all around the same age."

Evan reached for the scone and broke off another piece.

"Half of Jessica's fortune went to Henry and Kaye, because they were her sister Alice's kids," he continued after finishing the scone. "The other half will go to nine cousins, plus my Ivy. She dropped Gina, Zoe, and Reggie after their prank, and she changed the Spencer Industries bylaws so that they can never receive income from the mines."

"Did the message explain why she included Ivy?" Aunt Ferna asked in a quiet voice.

Evan nodded, staring down at the floor. "They all know she's a cousin, now."

Cora had never seen this side of Evan. Usually, he was full of bravado and bluster.

"Oh dear," Aunt Ferna murmured. "I almost feel sorry for those three. Even on her best behavior, Jessica could be quite difficult."

"So, the reason for the fight yesterday had to do with Jessica's will and the personal messages sent out by the attorneys," Cora said, her brows furrowed. "Wasn't that a little early?"

"No. It was per Jessica's will," Evan replied. "I didn't attend the reception. What fight are you talking about?"

"Gina, Zoe, and Willow got into a shouting match," Cora explained. "Their brothers jumped in to help, but the shouting didn't stop until the parents got involved."

"Did you say Willow?" Evan asked. "She and her brother will receive an equal share in Jessica's will."

"I think Gina or Zoe was trying to blame Willow and Arthur for being cut out of the will," Cora said. "It was all very confusing."

"But haven't we known all along that the murderer had to have been one of those cousins?" Aunt Ferna asked.

"It could've also been their parents," Cora suggested. "So that would include Lori, Walter, and the rest of them."

"I talked to a few of their parents about any entanglements with Nick," Evan said. "But they mostly seemed offended by the idea, feeling he was too young."

"To be fair, with this change in the will, I think we can narrow the suspects down to Zoe, Gina, and Reggie." She turned to Evan. "Do you know if those three will receive their income from Spencer Industries now that Jessica has passed?"

"Definitely not," he said. "They have no income and no inheritance. But their parents still receive an income and will probably support them."

"Something doesn't make sense," Cora said, her thoughts swirling. "With Jessica dead, they receive nothing."

"But did they know that?" Evan asked. "The only thing everyone knew was that those three had no income."

"Also, it was those three who performed that prank by roping in Willow and Arthur," Cora pointed out, leaning forward. "What if this is the same thing? Willow and Arthur didn't understand the prank, and they may not have understood their involvement in the murder."

"Oh..." Evan said, his eyes widening. "I hadn't considered that."

A moment of quiet elapsed.

"They killed her for the credits?" Aunt Ferna asked, shaking her head. "I don't believe it. I've known them all since they were children."

"Also, I understand why Nick couldn't figure out which one of them was the actual murderer," Cora said. "They seem to always act as a set. They move together, they play in a group, they spend a lot of time as a gang. If Nick was stumped, and he was their friend, I don't know how I'm going to figure out which one was the actual murderer."

"Maybe it was all of them." Evan slowly exhaled. "There's so much evidence framing Ivy. It's hard to believe one person orchestrated all of that."

"I know, I've thought of that, too," Cora agreed. "It might have been all of them acting together. I also wonder how the respirator tool fits into all of this. Did one of them use it on the barge? Then how did they get Nick's DNA on it?"

"I think this is too complicated for any one of them," Aunt Ferna said. "They must've been working together, even though I still can't believe it."

"But right now, I'm completely out of ideas," Cora admitted. "Maybe if I can find out more about the will..."

"Well, Captain Donaldson has a complete copy," Evan said. "He forwarded it to Redcliffe."

"Can you get a copy for me?" Cora asked.

"Probably," Evan said hesitantly. "Ivy's mentioned in the will, but you're not. So I don't know if they'd give you a copy. Let me contact Redcliffe and see what I can do."

In the middle of the afternoon, Aunt Ferna and Cora sat in their suite drinking afternoon tea. Halfway through, Brian contacted Cora, and a floating screen appeared above the table opposite her and Aunt Ferna.

"I hope I'm not interrupting," Brian said with a jovial smile.

"Oh, it's not a problem," Cora replied, speaking around a mouthful of teacake. "How are things going with Albright now that the funeral's over?"

"Things are going well," Brian said, his grin widening. "I got a copy of the will. Well, not the whole will—only the parts that pertained to Albright Corporation. Basically, all the changes Henry and Kyle put into place were correct. But there's one new thing—we have direct communication with the troops protecting our mines. Not the Spencer mines, which is fine. So, if we need more troops to cover one mine because of a potential threat, they'll accommodate us now. Henry did warn me, though, not to give too many commands, because the instructions could interfere with the troops' security plans, which they tailor to each site."

"That sounds like good news," Cora said, turning to Aunt Ferna.

"Congratulations," Aunt Ferna said warmly. "You've been managing Albright Corp very well. It reminds me of Benjamin when he was part of the management team. I know you'll do a very good job in the future."

Brian managed to stammer out, "Thank you, Aunt Ferna." He shifted in his seat. "So, how are things going up there?"

"Oh, about the same," Cora said. "Jessica's will cut off three Spencer cousins."

"That sounds like a clear motive," Brian said.

"Sort of," Cora said, running a hand through her curls. "There's a chance three of them may have roped in two more who didn't understand what was happening."

"Who are we talking about?" he asked.

"Gina, Reggie, and Zoe may have tricked Willow and Arthur into helping them kill Jessica. They were Jessica's second cousins."

"Oh yes, I remember them," Brian said.

"We think they did this before they knew what was in the will. In fact, if they'd known they were already out of the will, there'd be no reason to kill her."

"What I think we should do is take this new information to the EGS," Aunt Ferna suggested.

"I have a feeling the EGS already knows," Cora said, her words halting. "But it won't hurt to tell them, anyway." She sighed. "Based on my experience with the EGS, if they don't have clear evidence, they won't do anything about the new information."

"So where does that leave things now?" Brian asked.

"Right now, I'm completely stuck," Cora said with a sigh. "I can't figure out which one of them hated Jessica the most."

CHAPTER 18

The following afternoon, Cora and Aunt Ferna made their way to the space station's shopping floor. Cora wore comfortable black shoes, preparing for extensive walking. This contrasted with Aunt Ferna's more fashionable dusty-pink dress and matching tight shoes. They weaved around other shoppers on the crowded floor, but Aunt Ferna persisted, wanting to purchase some trinkets for her friends. Soft, colorful lights illuminated the storefronts on each side of the walkway. They passed high-end dress shops and gawked at beautiful, intricate hats worn mostly by older women at tea parties.

"Wow," Cora said, gaping at a storefront displaying personalized spacesuits. "They're lovely."

"Yes, dear," Aunt Ferna said, studying the same window. "But why would you personalize something so functional?"

"True, it doesn't make sense," Cora said, mesmerized. "But it's beautiful how they've used additional spacesuit material to create a layer of lace." She gasped. "You could get married in that."

"I suppose," Aunt Ferna said, pursing her lips. "Let's keep going."

They continued to the next few storefronts until they found a crystal store. These crystals, made from several minerals, were arranged by artists into soft, flowing shapes that resembled flower petals or feathers. Aunt Ferna grinned as she stepped into the store, while Cora groaned, realizing she was going to be in there for a while.

"Oh my dear," Aunt Ferna said, pointing at a new item. The artist had arranged crystals to look like an open field filled with a cacophony of flowers. "I think Mabel would love this."

"Yes, it's beautiful," Cora said, nodding her head. She stepped past her aunt to another display, eyeing rows of crystals arranged as rabbits, cats, and other furry animals, marveling at the artist's skill.

"Don't worry, dear, we won't be in here much longer," Aunt Ferna said, taking two steps forward and pausing again to examine another display.

Cora slowly made her way through the store, casually glancing at the crystal arrangements. After she'd seen enough, she found her aunt.

"Auntie, if you don't mind, I'll wait outside on one of the benches," Cora said.

"No, no, don't go! I'm nearly done now," Aunt Ferna said, placing several crystal creations into her basket. "This is for Mabel, Bertha, and Stacy. I just need one more."

Cora sighed. She'd heard her aunt say that many times before.

"Okay, I know, I know," Aunt Ferna said with a lopsided smile. "We can go now. I've picked everything out." She stepped to a side counter with her purchases. A robot gift-wrapped the crystals and placed them in a bag. Payment was automatically processed through comm bracelets.

"Where would you like to go now?" Aunt Ferna asked as they exited the store.

"I was kind of thinking of a cup of coffee," Cora said with a smile.

"I know the best place to go," Aunt Ferna said, pushing back her shoulders. "Follow me."

She marched straight across the walkway, causing several people to come to an abrupt stop to avoid running into her. Cora winced several times. She'd seen her aunt do this more than once and wondered how she managed not to run into anybody. Next, they turned and followed the flow of walkers back in the direction they'd come. After passing a few storefronts, they found the Martian Coffee Shop.

"I saw this on our way to the crystal store," Cora said. "I was kind of curious."

"Me too. I wonder if they use coffee beans grown in Martian soil," Aunt Ferna said, stepping into the store and grabbing a seat.

"I only want black coffee," Cora said as she sat down.

"What? No cookies? Teacakes? Sandwiches?" Aunt Ferna said with a sly smile.

"Well, maybe I could force something down," Cora said in a bubbly voice.

Cora ordered her black coffee along with a cinnamon teacake from the meal crafter, which materialized directly in front of her. Aunt Ferna ordered afternoon tea with a slice of strawberry layer cake.

"This smells amazing," Cora said as the waves of warm cinnamon wafted toward her.

"I know! I can smell your teacake," Aunt Ferna said.

They both ate in silence for a moment. After Cora finished her plate, she downed the last of her coffee. Leaning back in her chair, she sighed with a small smile.

"Better?" Aunt Ferna asked.

"I think we both needed afternoon tea," Cora said, sighing. "But my main problem has come back to me. I don't know how to continue Nick's investigation."

"Are you sure you should continue? It seems to me his efforts alerted the murderer and got him killed. Maybe you should do something completely different."

"What you're saying makes sense. But I can't even imagine what else I would do."

"Well, I'm sure you'll figure it out," Aunt Ferna said, taking another sip of tea.

"Wait a minute," Cora said. "You're always the one encouraging me to stop investigating or go to the EGS or something. What's different now?"

Aunt Ferna didn't answer right away. Instead, she swallowed more tea and then slowly lowered her cup back onto the table.

"It frightens me when you do one of your investigations," Aunt Ferna said in a quiet voice. "At the same time, you get results. I don't believe the EGS would have solved any of the previous crimes without your help. I really don't want you to conduct inquiries, but even I can see you're doing good work. You're keeping people safe, and I'm very proud of you."

Cora blinked, gazing at her aunt. She'd heard her aunt say she was proud of her for her schoolwork, launching a personal business, and even running the family mining operation. But Cora had never heard her say she was proud of her for the investigations.

"Thank you, Aunt," Cora said in a thick voice. "It means a lot to me."

"I think the problem is that you need to get a different perspective," Aunt Ferna said. "It doesn't change the fact that I want you to be careful. I still don't want anybody to harm my sweet Cora."

"You haven't called me that since I was a little girl," Cora said with a chuckle.

"Well, maybe I should say it more often," Aunt Ferna said with a gentle smile.

"I promise to be careful. I'll also rely more on the EGS for safety."

A moment later, both ladies stood and made their way to the antigrav lifts as they headed to their suite. Cora's comm chimed.

"Oh, it's Captain Donaldson," Cora said. "Would you mind if I took this?"

"Of course not, dear. I'll just take a moment to peek in here," Aunt Ferna said, ducking into a shoe shop.

Cora found an empty bench outside the shoe store and launched a vidchat with Captain Donaldson.

"Hello, Cora," Donaldson said. "You seem to be shopping."

"Yeah, my aunt wanted to purchase gifts for some friends," Cora said.

"Do you have time this afternoon?" the captain asked.

"What's this about?"

"Redcliffe has a few clarifying questions," he replied.

"We've finished shopping," Cora said. "I could be there in a few."

"Yes, if you don't mind, that'd help."

Cora closed the floating screen, wondering what Redcliffe wanted.

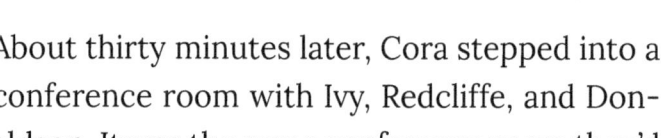

About thirty minutes later, Cora stepped into a conference room with Ivy, Redcliffe, and Donaldson. It was the same conference room they'd used earlier, which was significantly more comfortable than the interrogation room.

"Where's Evan?" Cora asked, surprised that he would miss a meeting that involved Ivy.

"He had a business meeting that he couldn't get out of," Captain Donaldson said. "In any case, this is really to clarify some points of your statement."

"Sure, ask anything you'd like," Cora said, reaching for the meal crafter, selecting a glass of water, and taking a swallow.

"Mr. Perry invited you on the spacewalk as a witness," Redcliffe said. "What or who were you supposed to be watching?"

"He was vague about that," Cora said. "I thought he wanted me to watch the group he usually hung around with, but he never said what to watch for."

Redcliffe nodded and took notes on a floating screen.

"When Mr. Perry's body first came into view, did you notice anyone else around you?" Redcliffe asked.

"There were people around me, although not close to me," Cora said, squeezing her eyes shut for a moment. "I didn't recognize any of them, actually."

"We were wondering who could have gotten close enough to Mr. Perry to sabotage his suit," Redcliffe said.

"Yes, and it was in a dead spot for the cams on the outside of the space station," Cora said. "Really, it was so shocking to see somebody float in front of me untethered. You could ask the assistant. I think his name was Richards."

"We did," Donaldson said. "He confirmed there was no one around you."

"I see," Cora sighed.

"Did you notice anything unusual about Mr. Perry's suit?" Redcliffe asked.

"No, what do you mean?" Cora said.

"We wondered if Mr. Perry's spacesuit had been damaged," Redcliffe said. "It seems unlikely someone had gotten close enough to disable his suit."

"I see what you mean, but I've been going down another trail," Cora said. She knit her eyebrows as something jogged a memory. Turning to Ivy, she asked, "If I give you a list from the friend group, would you tell me which ones are Viewers?"

Ivy nodded, a serious expression on her face.

"Let's start with you," Cora asked. "Your mom's a Viewer, right?"

"Yes," Ivy said. "The Santos family are all Viewers, but I'm not. I'm a Mover."

Ivy stared at Cora's glass of water, which lifted off the table and floated toward Ivy, who reached out and gently grasped it.

Cora nodded, then reached her hand out in the shape of a cup. Ivy let go of the glass, which remained in midair, and using her Mover abilities, made the glass float directly into Cora's hand.

"You have excellent control," Cora said with a small smile, lowering the glass to the table.

"Thank you," Ivy said, turning a little pink. "Uncle sent me to the best tutors."

"I already know that Evan is your dad," Cora said flatly.

"Sorry," Ivy said, chuckling. "I told Dad it was a bad idea to continue calling him 'uncle.' Everybody would discover the truth, eventually. The EGS figured it out right away."

Cora glanced at Captain Donaldson, who shrugged.

"Okay, let's continue," Cora said. "How about Gina Spencer?"

"Yes, she's a Viewer," Ivy said. "She can see long distances, like the surface of Mars or underneath Jupiter's atmosphere. There's a rumor she can somehow manipulate energy waves, which can influence a person's mind. But I've never heard her talk about it."

"Really?" Cora said with raised eyebrows. "I wondered exactly how her ability worked."

"Zoe's ability is stronger and a little different," Ivy said, pursing her lips.

"How does it work?" Cora asked.

"Zoe can actually put images in your mind," Ivy said with a small shiver. "Hers is the scariest because you can't tell what's real."

"Interesting," Cora said, pausing to gather her thoughts. "What about Reggie?"

"He's a Reader, like the other Spencers," Ivy said with wrinkled eyebrows. "But powerful. He can put thoughts in your head that aren't yours. But he's also very decent. I can't see him doing

any harm unless he was trying to defend someone."

"Like his sister?" Cora asked with a raised
eyebrow.

Ivy nodded.

"What about Willow?"

"She's a Reader, like Reggie. They have the
same abilities."

"How about Arthur?"

"He's a Viewer," Ivy said hesitantly. "I don't
know too much about his abilities, but I think
they might be fairly weak. He never talks about
it. I'm not sure."

"So, Reggie and Willow are Readers who can
put thoughts in others' minds," Cora said.

Ivy nodded and asked, "How is this related to
Nick's death? Did someone use the respirator
tool to make it so he couldn't breathe?"

"Yes, that's the EGS's working hypothesis,"
Cora said. "But I thought there might be another way of analyzing the evidence. Nick was
working on something, and I'm trying to pick up
his trail."

"Can you elaborate on what you're thinking
about?" Redcliffe asked.

"It's not a fully formed thought yet," Cora said.
"But I'll let you all know when I have a solid

idea." She paused, turning back to Ivy. "Let's see. Have I missed anybody? So, there are two Readers, Reggie and Willow. The remaining three are Viewers."

"What if we eliminate the weak Readers and Viewers?" Donaldson said. "That leaves Zoe, Gina, Reggie, and Willow."

"That doesn't narrow things down enough," Cora said, running a hand through her curls. "Can you tell me a little about their parents?"

"Well, you know Dad. My mom's Leatha, and she's a Viewer," Ivy said.

Cora nodded.

"Willow and Arthur's parents are Paul, who is a Reader, and Beatrice, who has no abilities," Ivy said. "But her mom was a Viewer. She was a Santos from my family. Gina and Reggie's mom, Terry, is a Reader, and Silas was a Viewer, but he passed away."

"And Zoe's parents?" Cora asked.

"Lori is a Reader, like all the Spencers," Ivy said. "But Walter is a Viewer. Only there's something unstable about him. He becomes angry so quickly."

Cora reflected on that argument between Zoe, Gina, and Willow. Walter had threatened Arthur, who was only defending his sister.

"Where are you going with all these questions?" Redcliffe asked.

"I'm trying to figure out which one of that group was capable of killing Jessica and Nick," Cora said. "A Reader could have also caused Nick to do something to himself, like use the respirator tool to disable the breather or open his own spacesuit, for example."

Captain Donaldson shifted uncomfortably in his seat.

Cora raised an eyebrow as she stared pointedly at him.

"I can't comment," the captain said in a firm voice.

"I don't think anyone in that group knew Jessica had changed her will," Cora said. "They could've killed her, expecting an inheritance." She turned to the captain again.

He cleared his throat. "Do you have any more questions for Ms. Santos?"

"No. Thank you, Ivy," Cora said, sighing with a sinking feeling and realizing what her next steps should be.

A floating robot arrived to escort Ivy from the room, but Donaldson, Redcliffe, and Cora remained seated.

"I wonder if you could do a little digging for me," Cora asked.

"What would you like to know?" the captain asked.

"Could you get more background information on the Spencers? I mean Gina, Reggie, Zoe, Willow, and Arthur," Cora said.

"Let me know what you find out, too," Redcliffe said.

They continued their conversation for a few more minutes before Cora left for her suite.

I might know what happened to Jessica and Nick, she thought, her mouth set in a line.

CHAPTER 19

The following day, Cora paced around a sofa in Evan's suite. She'd dressed in a business-casual blouse and skirt, feeling as if she might need a little psychological armor. It was the afternoon, and Willow, Arthur, Gina, Reggie, and Zoe sat at his dining room table, fiddling with floating screens connected to the Net. Evan, wearing his usual business jumpsuit, stood at the head of the table, glaring at the five people sitting around it.

"I invited you here to discuss Jessica's will," Evan said, barely masking his irritation. "Jessica removed three of you from her will but, for some reason, didn't tell you."

"You're not saying she left us credits?" Gina said, perking up.

Cora normally maintained her shield in a room with this many people, but she needed to catch a liar. She lowered her shield in tiny increments.

"Definitely not!" Evan said in a clipped tone. "She asked me to consider extending some credits to you from Ivy's inheritance if any of you were repentant."

"How many credits?" Zoe asked, closing her screen.

"It all depends on how you answer our questions," Evan said, his mouth set in a grim line.

"That must be one of the conditions for Ivy to receive her inheritance," Reggie said, sitting up a little straighter. His screen was already gone.

"Okay, well, we have nothing to hide," Willow said. "What's this about?"

Evan turned to Cora and stepped away from the table.

"We're checking into Nick's death," Cora said, pacing toward the table. "There are just a few things we want to understand." She reached the table and paused. "Which one of you was actually dating Nick?"

All five of them peered at each other, while Gina shifted in her seat. Willow reached for the meal crafter and selected a glass of water that materialized in front of her.

Cora sensed their tumbling emotions but couldn't tell what that meant.

"As far as I can tell, he had relations with my sister, Zoe, and Willow," Reggie said, bitterness edging his voice.

"No," Willow and Arthur said simultaneously.

"I went on a couple of dates with him years ago," Willow said. "I realized pretty early on he'd never stay loyal."

"But you were always very friendly with him," Zoe said with a sly smile.

"I could be friendly and not jump into bed with him," Willow said in a condescending tone.

"I don't think I've seen this side of you before, Willow," Gina said with a snicker.

"I'm tired of the constant barbs," Willow said, glaring at Zoe.

"Does that mean you two were both dating him?" Cora asked, pointing at Zoe and Willow.

"It's none of your business," Zoe spat out.

"When he was dating Aunt Jessica, he was loyal to her," Gina said in a weary voice. "It didn't stop Zoe from throwing herself at him, though."

Zoe hit Gina's shoulder.

"Ouch!" Gina said, rubbing her shoulder.

"You don't have to tell her everything," Zoe said in a curt voice.

"I need the credits," Gina said. "I'm not rich like you."

"Which one of you was in a relationship with Nick after Jessica passed?" Cora asked.

Zoe crossed her arms and studied a painting on the wall.

"It was Zoe," Gina said, popping out of her chair when Zoe tried to hit her again. Gina paced around the table and grabbed another chair next to Arthur.

"What exactly is the purpose of these questions?" Zoe asked, her face pinched in anger. "Do I need to get an attorney?"

"If you'd like an attorney, we can continue this line of questioning on the EGS floor," Evan said. "Would that make you more comfortable?"

Zoe huffed but didn't reply.

"I'm trying to answer three questions," Cora said. "One, who killed Jessica and Nick? Two, how did this person kill them? Three, why kill them?"

"Isn't this a job for the EGS?" Gina said. "How does solving a murder get us more credits?"

"The EGS is following another line of questioning," Cora said, congratulating herself for finding polite words to say that the EGS is solely focused on Ivy. "Maybe Jessica died so the murderer could … form relations with Nick."

"What!" Arthur said, popping to his feet. "Nobody would kill Aunt Jessica for something so silly, not even Zoe."

"Hang on, hang on," Cora said, raising both hands. "There'd be no reason to kill Jessica to get Nick and then turn around and murder him, too. So let's forget the why question. How was Nick murdered?"

"Someone sabotaged his spacesuit," Zoe said, glancing at the others, who nodded. "It was that tool thingy."

"We now know from the EGS it was suicide," Cora said, although this wasn't strictly true.

All five of them gasped.

Cora sensed their genuine surprise. It could mean they believed someone sabotaged Nick's suit, or the killer was surprised the EGS figured it out.

"It's possible for a Reader and a Viewer to influence a person's mind, causing them to harm themselves," Cora said, studying each of their faces. "But that requires a fairly powerful Viewer or Reader. And I believe that still includes all of you."

Zoe and Gina both peeked at Arthur before turning back to Cora. Reggie examined the crafter's menu. But Willow squeezed Arthur's hand. Cora understood that Arthur really was the weaker Viewer and not likely to be the murderer. But he could have helped.

"I don't understand why we're talking about this," Reggie said. "If one of us influenced Nick's mind, causing him to commit suicide, what sort of evidence would the EGS even have? No cams would capture our abilities when we're using them."

"Remember, you're helping Evan sort out events for extra credits," Cora said. She paused, selecting a glass of water from the crafter.

Willow and Arthur both selected tea and mini chocolate croissants.

"The EGS found the missing respirator tool used to disable the suit's air supply," Cora said. "It was still attached to his belt, and an autopsy revealed that only Nick had operated the missing tool."

"You really think one of us murdered Nick?" Arthur asked with pursed lips.

All five of them spoke at once, their anger piqued by the suggestion, and Cora considered raising her shield again.

"Quiet!" Evan said in a loud voice. All five jumped and turned to him.

"All the EGS's evidence either points to Ivy or Nick," Cora said. "You're all safe. This conversation is for the credits."

Evan stood to the side.

"Now, let's go into Jessica's passing," Cora said. "In the vids, I saw a knife fly off her desk and stab her in the chest. What could have done that?"

"A Mover, obviously," Willow said matter-of-factly.

"True, and the EGS tracking data puts Ivy, who's a Mover, in the room at that time," Cora said. "But if we examine things a little closer, there's the issue of the tracking armor. Somebody using tracking armor could have entered the room and stabbed her. The obvious question is, why couldn't Jessica see them? Tracking data only obscures surveillance equipment."

"That points to me, Zoe, and Willow," Reggie said in a quiet voice. "We're the only three who can influence others' minds with our abilities."

Willow shivered.

"But Gina's a Viewer," Arthur said, pointing at her.

"My abilities don't work like that," Gina said. "I can see the surface of Jupiter and Saturn, but I can't send the image to you."

"But none of us would've done something like that," Willow said.

"A forensic test of the tracking armor showed no DNA," Cora said. "But the EGS also did a detailed database search of the serial numbers attached to each part. Somebody from Lunar City purchased that tracking armor a couple of years ago. It was primarily used in the casinos. Ivy is from Heliton on Earth, but the three of you were born and raised in Lunar City."

The group at the table exchanged guilty looks.

So they all knew about the tracking armor, Cora thought.

"Let's continue," she said, taking a sip of water. "The EGS performed a forensic sweep of Jessica's suite. They discovered an abundance of evidence, proving Ivy spent a lot of time in that room. Except it was inconsistent with the surveillance vids that showed where Ivy was before and after the murder. Also, the amount of evidence seemed to imply Ivy had been in that cabin for weeks or months."

"So someone's trying to implicate Ivy," Reggie said with a small smile. "I knew she was innocent."

"Then there's the issue of Ivy's comm," Cora continued. "Initially, she said she had forgotten it in her room. And the vids show when she entered, she wasn't wearing it. Then within a minute or two, she leaned down and picked it up."

"Maybe she had it in her pocket and it fell out," Gina said with a shrug.

"Except Ivy said it felt as if something or someone touched her leg," Cora said. "This caused her to bend down and find her comm."

"Ivy and Uncle Evan are both Movers," Willow said. "A Reader or Viewer could've manipulated them."

"But my brother wouldn't harm anyone," Gina said in a pinched voice.

Reggie gave her a wan smile.

"Let's continue," Cora said. "Why would somebody want to kill Jessica? I've known her most of my life, and she was ... unpleasant on a good day. I understand from Nick she'd changed, but I never saw that side of her."

Evan shifted from foot to foot, clearly wanting to say something.

"When most people had dealings with her, it was usually about credits or political power," Cora said. "She wielded a lot of both. I don't think this had to do with power. I think her murder was about credits."

Zoe crossed her arms while Gina rolled her eyes. Reggie studied something on the tabletop while Willow and Arthur gazed expectantly at Cora.

"Yesterday, I had a long talk with Captain Donaldson," Cora said. "I asked if he'd do a background check on all the Spencers here on the station. Imagine my shock when I discovered all of you're in huge amounts of debt. The way you all spoke a couple of weeks ago, I thought your parents supported you. Since my assumption was wrong, I refocused on my first idea that you all plotted together to kill Jessica."

Chapter 20

"What?!" Gina said, jumping to her feet. Her chair fell back with a loud thud. "We didn't like Aunt Jessica, but we'd still never hurt her."

"I analyzed their debt levels, too," Evan said, clearing his throat. "For most of them, it wasn't unusual for an Askov. In fact, it was very close to my family's debt levels."

"Really?!" Cora said, raising an eyebrow. "I'll take your word for it. In any case, I asked Captain Donaldson to dig deeper into Lunar City's debt. That's when the truly eye-opening information emerged."

Cora paused, studying the five people at the table. They all appeared relaxed and interested in her words. But she sensed brief, repressed spikes of panic from Gina, Reggie, and Zoe, as expected.

"I hope you're not planning to surprise us by telling us Zoe has a lot of debt," Gina said with a dismissive wave. "We all know about her debt. She's always in debt, even though her parents give her credits every week."

"But did you know two casino bosses have actually put a bounty on Zoe?" Cora asked. "Haven't you wondered why you've been spending so much time in Tymal? Was it Zoe's idea?"

Four confused faces turned to Zoe, who glanced around the room, looking as though she might bolt.

"So, let me paint a different picture for you," Cora said. "Zoe, Gina, and Reggie, I'm guessing you didn't know you weren't in Jessica's will anymore. Then Zoe convinced the two of you to come to the Spencer Space Station for Jessica's annual State of the Company address. She told you that you were going to beg Jessica to reinstate your quarterly incomes."

"Well, yes, that's all true," Gina admitted.

"Shut up!" Zoe snapped. "We don't have to tell her anything. She's not the EGS."

"But I thought we would get credits," Gina said, her voice nervous.

"You're so stupid," Zoe shot back, standing and leaning across the table at Gina. "This isn't about the credits. They're trying to prove we murdered Aunt Jessica and Nick."

Cora instinctively raised her shield against the heightened emotions.

"Well, I didn't kill Aunt Jessica," Gina said.

"Are you trying to say I did?" Zoe asked, crossing her arms. "I didn't do a thing to that old woman."

"Calm down, everyone," Cora said. "Please, have a seat."

She waited until they settled back into their chairs.

"Let me walk you through a scenario," Cora said. "When the three of you got here, you ran into Willow and Arthur. Their dad makes them attend every year. Who's idea was it to start including them in your trips to the pool, games floor, and casino?"

"Zoe's," Reggie said, turning to face her.

"On the day of Jessica's speech, all five of you attended," Cora continued.

They all nodded.

"Afterward, Willow and Arthur made it to the Observation Deck where Brian and I met them," Cora said. "Willow could've killed Jessica and then raced to the space station's top floor, but the timing would've been very tight."

"No, it couldn't have been Willow," Arthur said, frowning.

"It could've been her, but it was unlikely," Cora corrected him. "Anyway, the EGS tracks everybody's whereabouts on the space station all the time. Evan and Ivy went to meet some friends, and the surveillance vids caught them in a restaurant with several people. However, Ivy's comm, which was still in her room, started moving and entered Jessica's suite. Note that Zoe's comm never left her room."

All eyes turned to Zoe, whose face flushed, and she frantically shifted her gaze around the room.

"You just said my comm never left my room," Zoe said, her voice rising. "I didn't do it."

"I'm going to guess what happened," Cora said. "You used the tracking armor to make you appear as Ivy to the surveillance cams while wearing Ivy's comm and made your way to Jessica's suite. Using your Viewer abilities, you would've blended into any background if you ran into anyone in the hallway, lift, or Jessica's suite. You entered her room, stabbed her, then waited for Evan and Ivy."

"No, no, no," Gina said, her voice shaking. "Zoe is selfish, but she's not a cold-blooded murderer."

"Here's another idea," Cora said, pressing on. "Maybe you didn't realize Evan and Ivy had plans to meet Jessica and you nearly ran into them after the murder. You couldn't return Ivy's comm to her room because you needed it to appear as though Ivy was there earlier and then left. But the vids showed Ivy moments after you killed Jessica. You must've been panicked."

"I would never kill Aunt Jessica," Zoe said, her voice rising again. "This is ridiculous. Besides, you don't have any proof. And I don't have to sit here, I'm leaving right now." She jumped to her feet, spun on her heel, and headed for the door. She stopped just before reaching it.

"It's locked," Evan said, his voice firm. "It's not going to open again until we start getting some answers."

A moment of pure panic crossed Zoe's face as she turned her head in short, abrupt movements, scanning for an exit.

"What was your plan when you killed Jessica?" Cora asked.

"I didn't kill her," Zoe shouted, shaking her head.

Cora sighed.

"Where did you three go after Jessica's speech?" Evan asked.

"Reggie and I went to our rooms," Gina said. "But ... I really don't think Zoe killed Aunt Jessica."

"What about you, Zoe?" Cora asked.

"No, no, no," Zoe said, her eyes wide. "I didn't kill her."

"What I don't understand is how you could stab somebody in cold blood like that," Evan said.

"Argh!" Zoe stomped back to her chair. "I keep telling you all I did not kill her."

"But surely the EGS would've found the discrepancy between the surveillance vids and Ivy's comm?" Reggie asked.

"According to Captain Donaldson, when the EGS tracks you, they're really using your comm bracelet," Cora said. "A few days ago, they used the EGS's AI and sifted through hours of space station-wide vids to discover Ivy at a restaurant while her comm moved from her room to Jessica's."

Evan muttered something under his breath.

"When you think about a Viewer going after Nick, it makes sense," Willow said. "He had no abilities—he was completely defenseless."

"But Zoe loved Nick," Gina said. "She'd never hurt him. In fact, he hurt her many times."

"Shut up, Gina!" Zoe exploded, then burst into tears as she covered her face.

Gina stepped toward her and wrapped an arm around her, guiding her back to the table.

"Zoe, maybe it's time to tell the truth," Gina said, her voice gentle. "He hurt you so many times. Why did you let him back in your life?"

Zoe continued sobbing as Gina comforted her. After a moment, she wiped her tears and gazed at Cora.

"I killed him," Zoe said quietly, her voice breaking.

Cora almost felt sorry for her. But thinking of Nick and Jessica hardened her resolve.

"Somehow, he figured out I was the murderer," Zoe said. "I tried to explain that I had to kill Aunt Jessica for us, but he wouldn't listen." She sniffled. "But he said he never loved me, and he didn't even like me. Instead, he was going to turn me in to the EGS. I begged him to wait twenty-four hours so I could talk to an attorney and start the legal work. But really, I needed time to set up my plan."

"Did you plan the spacewalk to kill him?" Cora asked.

"No," Zoe said in a low voice. "That had been planned days earlier. But I needed time to figure out how to kill him. I've been coming here since I was a girl, and I know a lot about this station. I waited until he was between the cams. When I asked him to stop with me, he wanted to go back to the barge, but I had to detain him a little longer. After he lost consciousness, I opened his suit, and the air rushing out pushed him away from the station. I needed it to look like suicide."

"How could you do something so heinous?" Reggie asked.

"He shouldn't have made promises he didn't plan to keep," Gina said. "He hurt her so many times."

"That doesn't excuse a murder," Arthur said, his voice firm.

"I just want to understand something," Cora said. "Did you put images in Nick's head to make him kill himself?"

"No," Zoe said in a watery voice. "I put images in his head after Jessica died, just to play with him. Then he said he was going to turn me in, so I followed him around for a day to make sure he didn't go to the EGS. I didn't need to be near him to alter what he saw."

"What happened on the day he died?" Cora asked.

"I stole the respirator tool from storage early in the morning." Zoe shifted uncomfortably in her seat, then fell silent.

"Then what happened?" Evan asked, his voice stern.

Zoe jumped before answering him. "On the barge, I made myself invisible to him and reversed his respirator. Then I hid the tool on the back of his belt."

"Reversed?" Cora asked. "The respirator was removing oxygen from his suit?"

Zoe nodded, wiping her face.

Suddenly, the door to Evan's second bedroom slid open, and Agents Tate and Reed stepped into the room with Captain Donaldson following behind.

"I think we've heard enough now," Agent Tate said. "We kept the reversal of the respirator a secret. Only the killer would know that. We have enough to start the proceedings."

"No!" Zoe stood, her eyes wide, as the EGS agents approached. She squeezed her eyes shut and placed her hands on her temples.

Cora, already shielded, felt the first wave of Zoe's Viewer energy. Now that they were in the same room, Cora felt sharp stabs, like an ocean of pointy knives jabbing into her mind. The pain rivaled one of her cousin Oliver's attacks.

Zoe really is quite powerful, she thought.

Evan and Gina both gripped their temples, and Cora knew they were struggling to raise their shields, but with a strong Viewer like Zoe, it would be difficult. Reggie and Willow both groaned but appeared to be building their shields as well. The only exception was Arthur, who shouted once before collapsing to the floor.

The EGS agents, who wore neurowalls that protected their minds from Askovians, were unharmed. Agent Tate cornered Zoe, pressing something into her arm. Zoe lost consciousness and was maneuvered into a chair. Agent Reed took out an instrument Cora hadn't seen before.

"Arthur," Willow shouted after she'd recovered and rushed to her brother's side.

Agent Reed placed a shiny disk on Zoe's temple. A floating screen appeared over her body, and Reed configured it.

"Is that a neurowall?" Cora asked, cautiously stepping toward them. Watching this procedure reminded her of the steps another agent had taken to subdue other Askovians.

"Yes," Captain Donaldson said. "It's a new military-grade neurowall that will completely repress her Viewer abilities."

After a moment, Zoe blinked a couple of times. She appeared calm, but Cora knew it was the influence of the neurowall.

Evan removed a medipad, an automated medical device, from the wall and rushed to Arthur. He activated it, causing it to transform from a floating oval to a flat medical bed. Agent Reed and Evan placed Arthur on the medipad.

"He's probably in shock," Agent Reed said, configuring the medipad to heal Arthur.

"Is he going to be all right?" Willow asked, wringing her hands.

"Medipad cycle complete," a robotic voice said.

"The medipad's done all it can," Reed said. "But it will take a couple of days for him to fully recover. You may want to have him checked by one of our more advanced units."

Willow nodded as Arthur's eyes fluttered open.

The agents escorted a docile Zoe, followed by Gina and Reggie, to the lower EGS floor. Willow helped Arthur to their family's suite.

After they left, Cora and Evan stood alone in the suite.

"That was harder than I expected," Cora said. "I thought she'd start talking earlier."

"I still can't believe she did it," Evan said. "It was so senseless."

"People have killed for lesser reasons." Cora pursed her lips.

Chapter 21

A few days later, Brian, Cora, Aunt Ferna, Eliza, Evan, and Ivy sat in the backyard of Cora's home, Brimble House. They'd just finished lunch and were enjoying after-meal cups of coffee and tea. A warm breeze ruffled Cora's yellow dress as she chuckled at something Brian had whispered in her ear. A lull in the group's conversation followed.

"I have to admit, it's wonderful being back on solid ground and not caged up in a box anymore," Ivy said, her bright smile lighting up her face. "There were many nights when I thought I'd never be able to enjoy a beautiful garden, warm friendships, supportive family, and a freeing, deep breath."

"Well, everything's all right now," Evan said, grasping her hand with a gentle squeeze. "There were many nights I worried, too."

"I've had a long talk with Mom, too," Ivy added. "I can't wait until she's home."

"The EGS is very dogmatic in its processes," Evan said, shaking his head. "I had really hoped they might do a little extraordinary thinking."

"Well, some of them can do that," Cora chimed in with a small smile. "Donaldson was very helpful."

"He seemed to be the only one," Evan said. "Sometimes, I wonder how those agents trained."

"I see what you mean," Aunt Ferna said with a sigh. "I understand the need to train agents to follow procedures for their own protection. But it leads to many cases like this, where if nobody is thinking outside the evidence, they won't come to the correct conclusion."

"Well, I have to admit it's been very interesting hearing of your exploits, Cora," Eliza said. "You're much braver than I am."

Cora smiled and felt her cheeks grow warm. She couldn't think of anything to reply.

"I've always known my Cora was brave," Brian said with a lopsided smile. "But now, I'm looking forward to spending some time with her. Something's always coming up."

"Well, my dears, it seems things have calmed down now," Aunt Ferna said. "Perhaps focus on settling into a nice routine."

"I'm all for a routine," Eliza said. "There's been too much turmoil in our household for my taste."

"I agree with you," Brian said. "Speaking of which, I spoke to Dad yesterday. He's doing well. He's spending a lot of time with Omar and his girlfriend, Irene."

"I spoke to him, too," Eliza said. "They've been working their way through the ship's restaurants, but they'll be on Mars in about three more months. I'm glad that he's happy, but I wish Mom could be, too."

"But I thought she was busy," Aunt Ferna said. "She's visiting friends, shopping, and traveling locally, of course."

"She's doing everything she can to keep herself busy," Eliza said. "But I can tell she's deeply unhappy. The problem is she's also very stubborn and won't admit to Dad that she was wrong."

Cora enjoyed the sound of birds chirping during a second lull in their conversation.

"Do any of you know what's going to happen to Zoe?" Eliza asked.

"I'll tell you what will happen to her," Aunt Ferna said, putting her elbows on the table and leaning forward. "She's going to disappear into some EGS testing hole, and her family will never see her again. I tell you, we should do something about this. They keep making Askovians disappear."

"Aunt, it's not entirely true," Cora said. "Oliver disappeared, and I think the same will happen to Zoe. But Hazel didn't disappear, and neither did Gavin."

"First of all, Hazel had already lost her older brother to the EGS," Aunt Ferna said. "Her mom wasn't going to lose another child to them. She was better prepared than Zoe's parents. Also, Gavin isn't an Askovian. He possessed illegal tech that he used to commit murder. He'll be fine."

"Actually, that's not true," Cora said. "I've been keeping tabs on Gavin. He did disappear. After the trial, his family lost all contact with him. So the EGS is doing something, but it isn't restricted to Askovians."

"That's news to me," Brian said. "I wonder what they're doing with the people they make disappear."

"They should only be in prison," Evan said, his eyebrows furrowed. "But the issue is if the EGS is experimenting on them, nobody's going to stand up for the rights of murderers."

"I know my Oliver murdered two people," Aunt Ferna said in a firm voice, "but that doesn't mean he deserved to be mistreated and then killed."

"Killed?" Evan asked, his voice sharp. "How'd you even know that?"

"It's just something that I feel," Aunt Ferna said, reaching for her cup of tea and grimacing. She selected a button on the meal crafter, re-filled her tea, and took a sip.

"And you come from a Feeler family, so I be-lieve you when you say it's something you feel," Evan said. "On the other hand, I prefer to see actual evidence. I wonder if this is something I could probe by myself."

"How are you going to have time to do that, Dad?" Ivy asked. "You're literally trying to run the second-largest mining operation across three moons."

"Good point," Evan said, nodding. "Sometimes I overextend myself."

"I suppose you could hire help," Ivy said with pursed lips.

"No," Evan said. "Even if I hire somebody, I still need to monitor them. I don't have time for that."

"Then nobody will ever stand up for the captured," Aunt Ferna said. "I know, I know. They were all murderers. But whatever is happening to them will eventually reach the rest of us. I've seen little hints of it." She turned to Cora. "When we were in Lunar City, I didn't realize there were neurowalls for Askovians. There might be, say, Movers who may need protection from Viewers, Readers, or Feelers. Our society is going to change, and not for the best."

Everybody exchanged glances, except Aunt Ferna, who stared into the garden.

"Aunt, would it be okay if we switched to a happier topic?" Cora asked with a small smile. "I would like to hear about Ivy's latest exhibit at the Alinac."

Aunt Ferna nodded, and all eyes turned to Ivy.

"Oh, I haven't released it yet," Ivy said. "But it's meant to be a flower exhibit. I know that sounds mundane. But it's a showing of flowers from a microscopic view. My mom can see into objects down to the micromillimeter. I had her describe, to the best of her ability, what she was seeing because she can't put the images in my mind. So, using her descriptions, I created an entire portfolio. I display flowers grown in greenhouses, wild open fields, mountaintops, and seashores." Ivy grinned. "It was a passion project of mine, so I don't know if anybody's going to like it."

"I've seen your previous work," Brian said. "You always have a very unique perspective that draws me in. When will it be out?"

"I submitted the last painting yesterday," Ivy said. "It takes them about a month to get everything organized and then send out all the invitations for the first private showing."

"Well, I hope you've included us," Cora said with a bright smile.

"Of course! You're all invited," Ivy said.

"Well, I can't wait for the beautiful field of flowers," Cora said.

***

To enjoy more cozy mystery science fiction, pick up The Runaway Martian (https://katherinesbooks.com/runawaymartianamz/).

Please Leave an Honest Review

Authors thrive on reviews. These reviews help other readers decide whether to buy the book. To write a review, simply go back to the website where you purchased this book, provide a star rating, and add a couple of sentences explaining why you liked the book. Thank you for your review.

Review Link (https://katherinesbooks.com/spencer-review)

WOULD YOU LIKE ANOTHER SCI-FI WHODUNIT?

Want to know how it all began? Dive into *Short Stories from the Feeler Universe* (https://katherinesbooks.com/sci-fi-short-story/), and once you join my newsletter, read this thrilling short story from *The Feeler* series! This prequel takes you to the very beginning, where Cora uses her unique Feeler abilities to unravel a gripping whodunit.

Books

Standalone Books

The Puzzle Safe Mystery
https://katherinesbooks.com/psmamz
The Runaway Martian
https://katherinesbooks.com/runawaymartia
namz
***

The Feeler Series Books

The Feeler (Book 1)
katherinesbooks.com/feeler
Movers, Mines, and Murder (Book 2)
katherinesbooks.com/movers
Lunar Justice (Book 3)
katherinesbooks.com/lunarjustice
Spencer Legacy (Book 4)

katherinesbooks.com/spencerlegacy

ABOUT THE AUTHOR

K atherine is a science fiction author who spent nearly thirty years working as an engineer before retiring and turning to her life-long love of storytelling. She grew up devouring classic sci-fi, especially the works of Isaac Asimov, Arthur C. Clarke, and Ray Bradbury. As much as she adored those stories, she often felt something was missing.

Over time, her reading tastes broadened to include cozy mysteries, thrillers, and fantasy. Eventually she realized her ideal book would be a blend of the genres she loved most. The solution was obvious: write cross-genre stories that fuse the wonder of science fiction with the charm and puzzle-solving of cozy mystery.

Katherine lives in New England, where she spends her days writing, reading, and enjoying time with her family.